OPERATION WAR WHOOP

Other titles by Orval Wax

The Deilonium Trilogy:

The Malfunction, Book 1 of *The Deilonium Trilogy*
Robots and Renegades, Book 2 of *The Deilonium Trilogy*
Operation War Whoop, Book 3 of *The Deilonium Trilogy*

OPERATION WAR WHOOP

BOOK 3 OF THE DEILONIUM TRILOGY

ORVAL WAX

DIVING
BOY
BOOKS

OPERATION WAR WHOOP
Book 3 of The Deilonium Trilogy

Copyright © 2026 by Orval Wax

All rights reserved.

Diving Boy Books
PO Box 2476
McCall, ID US 83638
www.divingboybooks.com

ISBN 978-1-960283-12-2 (paperback)

Book cover by Kristin Eames
www.kristineames.com

Book 3 of The Deilonium Trilogy

Dear Reader,

Warning of possible triggers: animal death, robot death, battle violence, and human death.

The Deilonium Trilogy is the product of one humble writer's imagination. He has presented as artfully and honestly as he could a select few of the symbols and tropes found in the collective psychology of humanity as a whole. These are meant to entertain you and shed light on the human condition.

Please remember, you are entering a world of make believe. No actual animals, people, or even robots, have been abused or killed in the creation of this story.

Respectfully,
Orval Wax

OPERATION WAR WHOOP

1

Charlie

For folks with a weak stomach, a Tibetan sky burial can be a pretty gruesome business.

It's the human tendency of empathizing with the corpse that does it. Your standard model John or Jane Doe just can't help thinking about his or her own flesh and blood when laying eyes on the chopped and scattered pieces of someone else's flesh and blood. I was no stranger to death. Heck, most of my best friends were dead people, but even I had trouble with it some days.

The trick is to wrap your mind around the Buddhist concept of the body as nothing but a tin can for the soul. That's what my pal Dawa was always telling me. He was good at it. He'd laugh at me when I'd gag while carving up cadavers at the *jhator* stone.

"Look at it this way," he'd tell me as the vultures bellied up to our ghastly lunch counter. "You and me are just little old ladies feeding birds in the park." He'd shake a femur at me and grin. "You have to remind yourself that at this point in the game, this stuff is nothing but a carbon compound."

I understood what he was getting at. From a rational standpoint, anyway. And yet, the thing I could never quite forget is that this lifeless lump of rigor mortis we were dismantling once had hopes and dreams.

It had loved someone.

Probably someone had loved it back.

Some mother or brother or mate.

I'm not saying that was necessarily a good thing. On the whole, love largely stinks. God knows I was done with that whole soul-crushing sufferfest. Never again. But a guy can't help feeling pity for those of his fellow idiots who are still trying to live in that fairytale.

Dawa seemed immune to this way of thinking. He was my role model. With his sleeves rolled up and a smile on his face, he went about his job like a mechanic in a salvage yard. But then again, Dawa wasn't your typical monk. He had spent time in the States studying economics and chemical engineering. He'd taught himself English through the brain-polluting method of immersing himself in American pop culture. He'd only returned home to Tibet after he'd been granted a vision of the Big Picture.

"We're all just electrically charged particles in the continuum of a ginormous universe," he told me. "We're all interconnected. I always knew that was true intellectually, but I saw it so clearly in that moment. It was so liberating. You see, Charlie, we're each one of us nothing but a collection of cosmic smithereens with interrelational psychological baggage."

I was skeptical about Dawa's so-called enlightenment.

Especially when he told me it'd come to him while waiting in the checkout line at Walmart.

———

Cold dry snowflakes were blowing in the air that day, swirling down out of the black clouds swallowing up the Himalayan mountaintops. Prayer flags fluttered in the wind – about ten thousand of them stretched on strings over the burial ground like a gigantic multi-colored spiderweb.

I was busy cracking bones with a mallet, turning them into bite-sized snacks for the greedy vultures crowding around me. They kept plucking at my robe.

Cripes!

How the hell did I end up in this nightmare?

Believe me, that's a question I asked myself a dozen times a day.

According to my fellow monks, karma was to blame. This was just a slow vehicle turnout on a very long road – a high-speed motorway littered with roadkill from all the reckless moves I'd made throughout my whole sorry life. I didn't much care for that analogy, but it sounded about right. And although I had always considered all of that Eastern hokum to be nothing but a big crock of New Age Buddha shit, something in me hoped that by helping others on the way to their reincarnation, I might clean up my record. If I could prove myself useful in this grisly business of recycling souls, maybe I could finally pay for my sins, quit this gloomy pit stop, and live out my days with a clean conscience. At least that was my optimistic goal. The reason I stuck with it.

Yeah, I know. Pathetic.

Anyway, that's what I tried to focus on as I went about my work.

Chop chop, crack crack.

It's funny how smells take you back. And not always to places you'd expect. Blood, at least in large volumes, smells petroleum based. Like old motor oil leaking from the crankcase of my granddad's beater Chevy pickup. That world and time seemed light years away from the Tibetan Plateau. That life. I guess in a way I'd been reincarnated since then. I'd come into this world as an innocent cub, was transformed into a coldhearted robot killer, only to be reborn as a sad-sack monk who spent his days trying to forget his boyhood dreams of becoming a comic book hero.

The way was haunted by ghosts.

A mother and brother and mate.

Along with an assortment of friends and enemies.

Gazing into the sky, I recalled the weightless sensation of falling through clouds under a parachute. Not back to earth, as you might expect, but into my own personal limbo. That's what this place actually was for me. After running halfway around the world, this is where I'd finally landed. I could see it clearly now. Just like Dawa had seen his own vision, but without the cosmic sense of freedom.

One of the vultures squawked and hopped away from the others who were gorging themselves on the gore. She had scored a tasty tidbit and was sneaking away so she wouldn't have to share. The big gray scavenger waddled a few steps and flapped up onto a rock. A severed hand was dangling from her beak. She held it by the tip of the middle finger, with the other fingers folded down, so that it looked like it was flipping me off.

I couldn't help myself.

My human weakness got the better of me.

I automatically grasped my wrist, rubbing the stump where my own missing paw used to be.

The lifeless hand swung in the vulture's beak, mockingly, like a sick joke.

Finally, the big bird spread her wings and lifted off,

catching the wind and rising up and up into the sky. She soared for a while, turning circles over the roof of the world.

I watched her getting smaller and smaller, until she disappeared into the clouds.

Then I turned and retched.

2

Back at the monastery, Dawa and I read the obligatory passages from *The Tibetan Book of the Dead*, chanted a sacred song, ceremoniously burned our funeral robes, and then bathed in the celestial fountain.

I could never get the death off me. I'd scrub and rub, but it permeated my cells. Mr. Death had become who I was. Or I had become him. I could never decide which. At any rate, all that hobnobbing with cadavers had marked me as a bloodstained agent of the dead.

Yak butter lamps flickered in the corners of the steamy room.

A big mandala was painted on the wall above the cleansing pool.

Dawa stood under the spigot jutting from the center of the geometric design and let the water splash over his head while laughing and singing about how much he liked piña coladas and getting caught in the rain.

No, singing retro-American pop songs was not standard practice in a Tibetan monastery. In fact, it smacked of sacrilege. But Dawa didn't give a damn about reverence. He had too much perspective to ever buy into that tight-assed piety. Like most things taboo in the world, he believed irreverence was just a human notion imposed upon a universe that couldn't care less. I was still reevaluating my own views on the world's sacred cows – i.e., money, religion, power, and God – but I leaned towards Dawa's way of thinking.

That's the one thing I liked about this backwater. It gave me room to think. For the first time in years, I had the leisure and distance from the madness of the world to figure out how I really felt about things. This wasn't one of those showpiece monasteries overrun by phone-wielding tourists shooting videos of photogenic pilgrims. It was an off-grid blast from the past, shabby, humble, and forgotten, hidden away in a remote corner of some of the highest and emptiest mountains on the planet. There were only a handful of nomadic yak herders on the surrounding slopes, and one small village deep in the valley below us, but for the most part, this place was nothing but a rarely visited dot on the map. A desperado like me could lay low here without worry of the posse coming around. I earned my keep by milking the livestock and butchering the occasional corpse. With my shaved head and red robe, I blended in with the brotherhood. Even my skin was the same shade as that of a local holy man.

After my bath, I skipped supper and went to my cell.

Night swooped in with a storm.

The other fellas slept in a communal dorm room heated by a mudbrick stove fueled with smoldering yak dung, but I holed up in the attic. I lit a butter lamp and slapped my arms against my sides to get the circulation going. The room was squat, windowless, and about as cozy as the meat drawer in a refrigerator. Wind whistled through cracks in the wall. I shook the frost from my sleeping mat and lay down, pulling the quilt up to my chin. My teeth were chattering. My breath came out as puffs of fog.

"Come on, Bear Claw," I told myself. "Go into it. Become the cold."

As I watched the shadows playing over the ceiling, I imagined disembodied arms and legs covering up with snow out on the dark and stormy mountain. That's when the parade started. Right on cue. It was the same thing every night. A procession of all the dead people and grizzly bears and robots from my past. Some of them I had loved, some hated. Either way, sleep never came until I relived the demise of each and every one of them. It was my morbid equivalent for counting sheep.

I'll spare the details, but let's just say the show was a gratuitous montage of over-the-top special effects yanked right out of a low-budget slasher flick. The stuff of PTSD. Lots of exploding heads and chest cavities. While the other monks were downstairs praying for a peaceful, daisy-strewn path to Nirvana, I murmured an apologetic litany to the maimed and blood-splashed ghosts who haunted my life.

The replay always ended with that decisive act of chopping off my own hand. The last fatality on my kill list. As if it had been a living person in its own right. A sort of ornery sidekick, complete with a personality, who I had murdered by separating it from the continuity of my other limbs and guts and bones. Sure, it's kind of wacky to personify a hand, but after a while without it, my missing appendage had started seeming like a long-lost friend. Albeit one with whom I had a troubled relationship.

I had stroked my wife's hair with that hand.

I had also used it to kill her.

A shiver gripped my body. A cold sweat. Was it from the ice in my veins, or just another tremor of self-loathing? Either way, I'd endured this nightly march of ghouls enough times to know that there was no way I was going to be allowed into la-la-land until I fully relived that moment when me and my hand parted ways. It was like reviewing gritty surveillance footage playing over the screen of my mind's eye.

I watched the late great Charlie Bear Claw bringing the hatchet down surgically – *Chlunk!* – through his skin and bone.

I watched him leaping across the cabin and jumping from the plane.

I watched him in freefall, struggling into his parachute, and then quickly strapping a tourniquet around his wrist before he bled out, the shock wore off, and he realized what the hell he'd just done to himself.

As I was confronted with my ghastly midnight movie, a phantom pain shot through the empty place at the end of my arm.

Nausea overwhelmed me, fueling my hallucinations.

The attic was suddenly crowded with my ghosts shuffling out for the night. One by one, they faded into the walls, until there was only a single figure left.

He stepped out of the darkness to the foot of my bed,

leering down at me.

Lamplight lit his face.

I waited for him to melt into the icy air with the others, but he didn't.

Instead, he spoke.

"Good evening, Charlie." He smiled like a demon from the brave new world. "Long time no see."

That's when I realized he wasn't a ghost.

3

Lance

The hunter sighed and sat up in his bed, his countenance oddly relaxed.

"You don't seem surprised to see me," I said.

He laughed. "Nope. Nothing really surprises me anymore. But I am very disappointed. You can only mean trouble."

"I have traveled a long way to find you."

"And just how in the name of Bodhisattva did you do that anyway? I thought I'd covered my tracks pretty well."

"You have a tracking chip in your neck."

The hunter shook his head. "That was removed a long time ago."

"No, Charlie. That's what you were led to believe, but the device is still in place and fully functional."

He felt the side of his neck, probing the inch-long incision scar with his fingertips. "Cramer's idea?"

"Yes."

"That double-crossing bastard."

"Don't be angry with the colonel. His intention was to protect you."

The hunter sneered. "And keep tabs on me."

"Colonel Cramer thought there might come a time when

he would need to find you."

"And I suppose this is that time?"

I nodded.

The man cursed through his teeth, but his demeanor was otherwise unthreatening. My character evaluation processor indicated that the individual before me was greatly depreciated from the fearless robot hunter who had once so ruthlessly tracked me down with the intention of terminating my life systems. Nevertheless, I was here on a mission and could not allow myself to be disappointed or distracted by his currently downgraded state of being. I slipped out of my backpack and sat cross-legged on the floor, initiating the purposeful conversation I had come so far to have with him.

"We need to talk, Charlie."

4

Charlie

"Don't get too comfortable, robot. State your business and scram."

"You don't have to be distrustful of me, Charlie. I'm here on friendly terms."

That made me laugh. "You'll have to forgive my bad manners, but I get cranky when uninvited guests interrupt my beauty sleep. Especially when that guest once tried very hard to murder me."

"I will remind you, Charlie, that you were malicious toward me long before I ever turned my aggressions on you. And what is more, I had done nothing to deserve your wrath."

He had a point. From his side of the story anyway. He also had the upper hand. No pun intended. Still, he didn't come across as armed or hostile.

"Much has changed in the last three years, Charlie." He studied me and then scanned my bachelor pad. "For both of us, apparently."

The condescending jerk.

And yet, I saw no reason not to believe him. Maybe this was just a friendly little visit from a kindhearted old rival – a chance for us to catch up, share some fun memories, and have a few laughs. Shucks, maybe he wasn't even here to kill me.

Sure, yeah, right.

"I've come on behalf of Colonel Cramer and his associates."

"Not that I give a rat's ass, but just who are those associates?"

"Obviously, I am one of them, but I am not at liberty to disclose the names of the others. For security reasons, the fewer details you know at this point, the better for everyone involved."

A lot certainly had changed if the colonel was now in cahoots with an android. The Cramer I knew had always lived by the credo that the only good robot was the one that had been decommissioned, dismantled, and melted down to make hubcaps.

"Here," said the bot. "This will tell you all you need to know."

He pulled a black metal box from his pack and handed it to me. I recognized it from my days working behind the lines as a warbot hunter. It was a hologram projector with security coding and encryption bypass protection. Cramer had sometimes used it to deliver messages to me in the field.

"The colonel said you would know how to access it."

My knee-jerk reaction was to hand the device back to the bot and politely tell him to stick it up his stainless-steel ass. That's what I should have done. Follow my instincts. Instead, like a damn fool, I hesitated. I examined it, turning it over in my hand. It brought back a lot of memories. Some of them pretty good. But the thing was a can of worms. I knew that well enough. And yet...

Curiosity is a curious thing.

Placing the box on the floor by my bed, I flipped open the lid and automatically punched in the eighty-three-figure sequence code. If I got a single digit wrong, the gizmo would self-destruct, torching me and the bot in a fiery explosion. But no chance of that. The code was tattooed on my memory like the phone number of an old high school sweetheart.

After the sequencing, I pressed the projector button, and a two-foot-tall 3D image materialized in the empty corner of the attic. It was of Colonel Donald Cramer standing in a well-lit room. The wall behind him was blank, made of interlocking steel panels of the type used by the military for constructing bunkers. There were no other clues to tell me where he was when he made the recording. They had taken pains to conceal their location.

As for the colonel himself…

It was startling to see how much Don had changed. He looked haggard. His hair had turned gray, and he was stooped to one side. He was wearing a cardigan sweater instead of a uniform. He was also wearing glasses. That was new. He looked more like a worn-out old granddad than a military commander at the top of his game.

The image flickered for a second, calibrating for transmission, and then the colonel spoke.

"Hello, Charlie. I'll keep this brief and to the point.

"The world is in danger in ways it never has been before. Björn Thorson has become a psychopathic monster intent on selectively wiping out life on the planet and then rebuilding it to serve his own interests. Unfortunately, he has developed the technology to do just that. I am working with a handful of people to stop him."

Cramer paused, removed his glasses, rubbed his eyes, and put them back on.

"Thorson has put into motion a series of procedures that will soon be irrevocable in their devastation. We are greatly outnumbered. Our enemy is far more technologically and militarily advanced than we are. Time is running out. They are closing in on us. I'm not sure how much longer we can stay hidden."

He cleared his throat and bobbed his head, looking directly into my eyes.

"I need you, Sergeant Bear Claw. Planet Earth needs you. You're the only one I know who can handle this. Frankly, your skills and primitive instincts are effective in ways that can get around modern combat systems. You're also the only one who understands what it feels like to be on the verge of extinction. The last Chompquaw. It may be too late for your tribe, Charlie. The People of the Bear. I'm sorry for that. But there's still time to save what remains of what you love – the mountains and rivers and forests, and the animals that live in them. If nothing else, I'm asking you to think of them.

"Lance will bring you to us, Charlie. You can trust him. He's on our team.

"I'll fill you in on the mission's details when you get here. Travel safe and keep your head down.

"Over and out closing sequence code 459 X Y Zulu 3843."

5

The holographic image buzzed once and evaporated.

I found myself staring into the dark empty air with the colonel's voice echoing in my head.

There was a chance that the broadcast was deep-faked, that it was some sort of trick, but it didn't feel that way, and I couldn't really come up with a good reason why it would be.

I sat there for a minute turning it over in my head.

The wind was blowing outside, buffeting the building.

Dawa and friends were sleeping downstairs.

Finally, Lance stood. "We need to leave now, Charlie. We can't afford to waste another minute."

I considered his words.

The robot opened his pack and pulled out some mountaineering togs and a pair of hiking boots. "These are for you," he said. "Put them on and let's go."

I remained motionless on my sleeping mat.

The bot let out an exasperated sigh. Uncannily human. "What are you waiting for?"

"Are you familiar with the Taoist philosophy of Wu Wei?" I asked him.

His expression went blank as he accessed his knowledge

banks, and then he answered, "The practice of active inaction."

"That's right. It's the idea of letting events play out without trying to change them."

"This is no time for that, Charlie."

"Who's to say?"

"The world is in danger!"

"Look, robot, I've spent my whole life pretending I'm some sort of tough guy on an all-important mission, but since I've been in this place, I've come to see things more clearly. I've been fighting something I can't beat. I've been punching and kicking at the inevitable evolution of our little corner of the universe. There's no way to stop it." I stared hard at the bot. "So maybe it's time for me to quit wasting my energy."

"This is not how Colonel Cramer describes you, Charlie." The bot shook his head. "And it is not in accordance with the character trait index coding that I have assigned to you either."

That tickled me. This bucket of bolts had a favorable opinion of me.

"We're talking about the end of the world, Charlie. Our team is trying to save the planet."

"Have you ever stopped to consider that Thorson might be right? Maybe our dear old Mother Earth is yesterday's news. I've been off grid for a while, but the last time I checked the zombie masses of humanity and the corrupt power-hungry, money-grubbing politicians they've put in charge care more about their precious economy than they do about their earthly home. They're more interested in subdividing the last open spaces with their oversized houses and filling them up with plastic junk than they are in doing what's needed to save the planet. Maybe it's time to unplug the old girl from life support, end her suffering, and just let her and everyone on her die."

"You don't believe that."

"Well, even if I don't, what does it matter? Have you taken a good look at me lately?" I held up my stump. "I'm not the Übermensch I used to be. I don't have the stomach for he-man heroism anymore. My get-up-and-go has got-up-and-left-town."

"Yes, I've noted your state of disrepair. Your physicality has been compromised, and your testosterone levels appear to be alarmingly low, but within the dynamo of your spirit, the spark of a fighter must surely remain."

I shrugged. "People change."

The bot was at a loss. The digital gearbox in his brain shifted into overdrive as he tried to come up with a convincing argument for why I should join his club.

"Why do you care so much anyway?" I asked. "You're a machine. You don't need fresh air and clean water to survive. Besides that, you're as much a part of the new order as anything there is. Just reprogram yourself and take your place in Thorson's bright shiny future. For crying out loud, robot, you're my replacement!"

The bot shot me a revealing look, and suddenly I could read him like a book. That tragic frown. The sad little wrinkles around his eyes. He might have been nothing but a fuse box in a pretty package, but at least something about him was pitiably human.

"Oh," I grinned. "I get it. This has something to do with that girly-bot you're so ga-ga over." I laughed. "She's really got you by the spark plug, doesn't she? Yeah. She's quite a gal. I might just have a crush on her too. How is our girl Moxie anyway?"

He stiffened. "My orders are to discuss nothing but our

mission, and only with a limited divulgence of its details."

I had obviously scratched a raw wire.

"Okay, Romeo. Have it your way. But in that case, I guess there's nothing left to talk about. It's been nice to see you. Let's do it again real soon. But now it's time for you to say goodnight."

He started to respond but only clenched his jaw.

I pointed to the exit. "Don't let the door hit you in the ass on your way out."

He stammered. "You do realize that Björn Thorson is still coming for you. He's getting close. Our intelligence gathering systems suggest that he has greatly reduced his search grid pattern for your location." He gestured to the snoozing monks downstairs. "You're putting innocent lives in danger, Charlie. You're being irresponsible."

"*Que sera, sera*," I said. "Whatever will be, will be."

I was still getting used to robots being so much like humans. Most of my experience was with behemoth combat units that looked and acted less like people and more like berserk backhoes armed with Torb canons and brip guns. It was both eerie and enjoyable to cause this bot so much frustration.

"Farewell, Captain Marvel," I said. "Good luck saving the world and may the force be with you."

"This behavior doesn't correspond with your previous actions," said the bot. "That day in Nairobi when Moxie took us on the Chameleon Hawk…"

"What about it"

"Your gesture…"

"You mean lopping off my own hand?"

He nodded. "There was a quality about that action that was so grand and fitting. And so ineffable. It reconfigured my opinion of you. I have since come to consider you an extraordinarily noble human being. I have come to believe that you are more than just an unscrupulous savage, but rather a person of exceptional integrity and grit."

"Sorry to disappoint."

The bot's face went all hangdog. Nothing was going right for him tonight.

"I am regretting that I ever bothered," he muttered.

"Bothered with what?"

He sighed, shook his head, and reached into his pack. "This is for you," he said, and handed me a tin can with a lid. "It was to be my own reciprocal gesture," he said, "one that might demonstrate my sincerity and show my change of heart since those days when I hunted you with the intention of your complete destruction."

I turned the can upside down, examining it. "What the hell is it?"

"A symbolic gift of gratitude," said the bot.

I waited for him to explain.

"It is a peace offering, Charlie. It's your hand."

6

Lance

The hunter expressed confusion as he regarded the metal cylinder in which I had packaged a portion of his mortal remains.

"I had your severed accessory cremated," I explained to him. "That is what many human cultures do with the bodies of their deceased loved ones, and although this is a slightly different scenario from that, my intention was to offer you a small-scale version of that experience so you might go through the grieving ritual which is so necessary for your species."

The hunter swallowed. "Robot…" he said. "I…"

"I meant to give you an opportunity for psychological closure, Charlie, as a way to pay you back for your selfless and poetic act."

His eyes glistened in the lamplight.

I let a moment pass, allowing the hunter to process his emotions.

"Well," he finally said. His voice was low and hoarse.

When he said no more, I shouldered my pack and prepared to go. "I wish you would join me on my mission, Charlie. I believe that by combining our skill sets and knowledge platforms, you and I could help Colonel Cramer defeat Björn Thorson and stop his destructive plans for the planet."

The hunter raised his gaze to mine. "I'm sorry, robot. I just don't have it in me anymore. The old fire is gone." He smiled sadly. "That part of me is dead."

His decision appeared to be irrevocable, and I saw no practical reason to waste any more time trying to convince him to change it. Seargent Charlie Bear Claw was officially out of commission and unavailable for combat.

Turning, I moved to the door. Just before I stepped through the exit, he called to me.

"Hold on, robot."

He held up the tin can.

I waited.

"I do appreciate it," he said. "I mean…" He shrugged. "It's weird as hell, but thanks, Lance."

I nodded summarily.

And then I left the man behind.

7

Charlie

After the bot left, I just sat there staring at that tin can. It stirred up some seriously confusing feelings. My head started humming with wild thoughts and memories, while my heart flip-flopped like a trout thrown out onto the muddy bank of a stream. It's one thing to hold an urn of, say, your departed mother's ashes. That sort of thing is expected. That's a natural step in the long march through the generations. But to hold a piece of your own dead self can really dip your rocks in ice water.

"Holy moly," I muttered. "Good grief."

And yet, I couldn't indulge the weirdness right now. If what Lance said was true, the clock was ticking. Thorson's kill squad was closing in on me. I needed to vacate the premises so Dawa and his fellow lotus-seekers didn't get caught in the crossfire.

One of the few perks of being a corpse-carver is that you always have access to a good sharp blade. Old habits being what they are, I kept one under my pillow. I slid it out of its case and sterilized it over the flame of the lamp. Guiding the blade to the old incision scar on my neck, I sliced into myself, wincing as the blade parted the skin. With only one hand to work with, it was an awkward operation, but I managed to expose the tracking device from where it was embedded in my flesh. I placed my makeshift scalpel on the floor, gritted my teeth, and pinched the cut, squeezing the pill-sized transmitter out of my neck.

I still had the trauma kit I had snagged when I jumped from the Chameleon Hawk on that fateful day three years earlier. All of the good stuff had been used up long ago, but rummaging through its Band-Aid wrappers and scraps of gauze, I found some suture tape and slapped it across the wound.

Blood trickled stickily inside the collar of my robe.

I held up the pellet in the lamplight and studied it. I couldn't decide if I was mad at Cramer for his treachery, or grateful.

Maybe a little of both.

As a friendly joke, Dawa had once given me a plastic figurine of a meditating Buddha who looked like Elvis Presley. He had picked it up as a souvenir in Las Vegas during his cultural tour of the U.S.A. I kept the kitschy thing on a shelf, and now I placed the tracking device in Elvis Buddha's lap. If the colonel's bunch ever cared to check in on me, I wanted them to think I was still in residence at the monastery. By the time they figured out the truth, I hoped to be well off their radar.

Lance had left the mountaineering clothes and boots behind. I dropped my robe and slipped them on. He also left the hologram projector. It was booby-trapped with incendiary explosives and not something we wanted falling into the wrong hands. I stuffed the projector into one of the pockets on my parka and then tucked the tin can with my pulverized hand into the other, zipping both pockets shut.

A wave of nostalgia smacked me hard as I gazed around the attic. I felt like a sentimental dope, but this place had been pretty important to regaining my sanity. I had done some healing here. At the very least, I had come to grips with some of my issues and accepted some hard truths about myself and my life. I didn't necessarily feel like the healing was complete, but too bad for me.

After snuffing out the butter lamp, I left the room behind.

8

Setting off in the middle of the night during a blizzard was not one of my more brilliant moves. The wind cut inside my hood, blasting my face with ice. I was knocked to my knees more than once as the gusts slammed against my back. I considered turning back and waiting for the weather to improve, but my gut told me I needed to get moving. If Lance and Co. could find me, Thorson's hoodlums couldn't be far behind.

Maybe I was just being an old school romantic – after all, every square inch of the planet was on view from Thorson's fleet of satellites and surveillance drones – but I approached my escape strategy in the style of a renegade redskin in an old western. The lowlands and passes were the most likely places for an ambush, so I'd stay high on the slopes and ridgelines. It was late winter. The traveling would be slow and dangerous, but no one would be looking for me up there in the rarefied air at the edge of the death zone.

That was my simple strategy as I floundered through the drifting snow.

But first I had to make a stop.

The wind moaned over the burial ground. The snow put off a ghostly glow, and I could just make out the dark shapes of prayer flags snapping on their lines.

I had launched a lot of souls from this site. If you were to believe the Buddhist boys I hung out with, anyway. But in all those ceremonies, I'd never performed a ritual quite so personal and confusing as this one. Don't get me wrong. I still hated robots. But I guess Lance's creepy little gift had moved me with its sentiment.

I decided to keep the ceremony simple. No prayers or incantations. Nothing mystical and maudlin. Just the cold hard reality of death. The rejoining of my altered carbon with the elements. Still, as I dug that tin urn out of my pocket and sheltered it with my body, I found myself strangely emotional. I was too thick between the ears to understand what was going on with me, but the moment felt pretty damn profound.

I clamped the can under my left arm and carefully unscrewed the lid. Then I lifted it up in the darkness.

In spite of my resolve to remain the hardened nihilist, I couldn't help myself.

I just had to say it.

"Katoyotapsommiki."

That sacred word left my lips as I turned the can upside down, letting it spill into the wind. Those ashes mingled with the Chompquaw language and the snowflakes and flew off across the Himalayas. They whirled up into the darkness, mixing with the storm. They drifted – I hoped unreasonably – as high as the heavens, across this whole wide world, and all the way back to my Yellowstone homeland.

And then they were gone.

Leaving me, a one-handed Indian, alone in a boneyard with an empty tin can.

———

I don't know how long I stood there.

Long enough for my joints to get stiff.

And long enough for my thoughts to get sluggish.

I might have stayed there all night if the storm hadn't blown itself out and disrupted my self-pity with its sudden change in barometric pressure. The wind dropped and the air became still. The clouds parted and a full moon appeared over the snowy landscape, shaking me from my torpor.

I lifted my face to the silent void and filled my lungs with a breath of cold blue moonlight.

"Okay, Bear Claw," I told myself. "Time to skedaddle."

I hadn't taken two steps when something caught my eye. Something glinting in the moonlit sky. Metallic, shaped like bullets, and moving fast. I counted six of them.

Missiles?

Angels?

Jets?

With a roar of displaced air, they dropped and cut low over the mountainside. That's when I saw them clearly.

Demonic.

Evil.

Warbots with wings!

9

I loped a few steps through the snow and then stopped. The monastery was a mile away and the warbots had already touched down and were making their assault. There wasn't a damn thing I could do but watch as Thorson's deadly machines descended upon the defenseless inhabitants.

It was like a macabre fireworks display. Explosions, bright colors, and the percussive whump of Torb rounds echoing over the hills and shaking me in my skin. I had seen my share of massacres over the years, but never one quite so nightmarish and lopsided. I was pretty certain I could hear, very faintly between the blasts, the cries and screams of dying monks.

Once the building was leveled, and everyone inside of it incinerated, the bots gathered at the edge of the smoking inferno like a gang of happy-go-lucky Nazis discussing where to go for an after-genocide beer. Indifferent to the carnage they'd just caused. Without any indication of human empathy and remorse. They must have received a signal from their control station right then, because they all fired their jet propulsion burners at once and hovered in formation a few meters off the ground.

Then they blasted off.

Their trajectory sent them my way and I quickly dropped and covered myself with snow. I lay on my back with my right eye exposed just enough to get a good view of the winged devils passing overhead.

So this is the fine art of Wu Wei, I thought as I lay there hiding. This is inaction in action.

I can't say that it felt very good.

It was definitely counter to my Chompquaw upbringing.

If I was being honest with myself, it felt like a cop-out.

But I was determined to stick with my new approach to life. What did it matter anyway? I couldn't change the inevitable. I was too ineffective. An old school caveman who wasn't up to speed with modern times. A fairytale hero who couldn't cut it in the real world.

I felt sick about Dawa and his buddies. Their only crime was unwittingly harboring a fugitive. That was a bad on me. Another pound of guilt to add to my already sagging load. But whatever will be, will be, right? Surely no one could understand and accept that better than a Tibetan monk.

Even then I knew I was kidding myself, cowering behind the flimsy walls of my crackpot philosophy. Over the past three years, I'd gotten pretty good at justifying my nonparticipation in the world's problems.

But deep inside I knew the truth.

Sure, Bear Claw. You're just so damn wise and vindicated.

Uh-huh. You bet.

Tell it to Dawa and those boys who'd just been so mercilessly blown to cosmic smithereens.

10

Lance

The muted thud of explosions syncopated with the red flashes pulsating above the ridge between my current location and the monastery 9.4 kilometers to the north. The evidence suggested that Björn Thorson's extermination squad had discovered Charlie Bear Claw's hiding place. Melancholy overwhelmed my emotions center at that realization. I had foolishly hoped to win the hunter as an ally. I had envisioned him and me saving the world together like, frankly, a pair of adventure novel action heroes. Instead, I had very possibly led the enemy to his doorstep. But I had no time to entertain my guilt and despondency right then. The world was in peril. I needed to report to Control and obtain procedural orders for my extraction so I could get back in the fight.

I pulled the communication device from my pack, dialed its frequency to the internal receiver of my auditory intake units, and then linked it to my voice capacitor before initiating the call.

"Commencing operational contact code Tango Tango Mike Bravo Whiskey Alpha Tango."

Four seconds elapsed before I received an answer, and then – "Enter personal verification code."

Even under the dire circumstances, I found it impossible to suppress the surge of elation I felt at hearing Moxie's voice on the other end of the transmission.

I entered my ID coding and waited to receive my orders.

In the meantime, the clamor of warfare subsided on the far side of the mountain. The flashes faded and the ridgeline became illuminated with moonbeams.

"Hello, Lance. Cramer here."

I could clearly picture the scene at the console. The colonel would be leaning over Moxie's shoulder while scanning the monitors and maps on the panel before them. The colonel's personal assistant, along with a few other members of the team, would be standing quietly in the background, waiting anxiously for my report.

"Evidently," said the colonel, "you were unable to convince Raider One to join our cause."

"Yes. That is true. How did you know?"

"Bear Claw's tracking device has stopped transmitting. Its final signal was sent from the monastery. Apparently, he was still on site when Thorson's forces arrived." The colonel gave a weighted and meaningful pause. "We can only assume the worst."

"I'm sorry," I replied. "I failed."

"No, Lance. Charlie was a good man, but he was headstrong and shellshocked. He'd been to hell and back, and was badly wounded, both physically and emotionally. I knew it was a long shot. I'd just hoped for a miracle."

After a moment of silent reverence for his fallen comrade, the colonel murmured, "Rest in peace, buddy," and then briefly discussed my rescue plan with Moxie before returning his attention to me.

"We need to keep this short, Lance, since we obviously

have a breach. There's no telling how close Thorson's forces are to discovering our location. They're possibly tracing our comms through our repeater stations and deciphering our global positioning algorithms."

"I understand."

"We have to assume you're hot, Lance. We have to assume they've got a fix on you and your movements."

That was discouraging news. It could only mean one thing.

"Sorry, Lance. You'll have to go black."

I sighed. "Copy that."

"Moxie will brief you on procedure. Good luck, Lance. I hope to see you soon."

Although I knew that the chances of that were slim, for the sake of the team, I intoned a deliberately upbeat tenor to my voice. "Thank you, Colonel."

He turned the speaker over to Moxie. "Okay, lover boy. Listen up."

The irony of her pet-name for me only made the moment more disheartening. Although I had originally been manufactured as an android unit designed for amorous interaction, and there was no one in the world with whom I'd rather share my talents than Moxie, I was in no way her lover boy. She had made that perfectly clear in the past.

"One question, Lance. The doctor wants to know if your power unit is still working properly."

"Affirmative. I have had no problems maintaining sufficient power levels."

"Great. Okay then. You will initiate Recourse Plan F7. I repeat, F7. Do you copy?"

Disappointment inundated my emotions processor. "Copy that," I replied. "Foxtrot 7."

"Proceed by variable route patterns as required for

concealment. Make no contact with base. Do you copy?"

"Yes," I answered. "No contact. Copy."

"Is there anything else we need to know before we break communications, Lance?"

I nodded in the moonlight. Yes! I thought. Yes! You need to know that I am doing this all for you, Moxie, all for you because I love you and hope to win your heart through my heroic actions so that we can someday live forever as mates in a paradise of our own making.

"No," I said. "I'm mission ready."

"All right then, lover boy. Keep that gorgeous kisser of yours off the bad guy's vector and maybe we'll see you again sometime."

"Roger that," I replied in the business-like manner of a soldier in the field. "Over and out."

Immediately, as per protocol, I set the timer on my portable transceiver and tossed it into the snow. After five seconds, the self-destruct mechanism detonated, reducing the device to a puff of smoke.

I was now officially on my own.

11

Charlie

Never second guess a maniac.

You can put that down as one of Charlie Bear Claw's hard-fast rules for survival.

And yet, all of the signs were telling me that I'd just been checked off Björn Thorson's to-do list. At least that's what I came up with when I did the math.

Warbots + Torb Canons = One Dead Indian

Honestly, I was surprised by how easy it had been to simply un-exist. The almighty jerk had obviously gotten careless since our last go round. Deploying his death machines to do a man's job was a sloppy tactic. Those bucket-headed dunderpates didn't even verify that I was physically on site before they let loose with their mayhem. Probably Lance had led them to me. Thorson's crew must have gotten a bead on the friendly skin job's movements. Although my field coding had always been secure in the past, maybe they'd found a way to tap into Lance's signal for the tracking device in Elvis Buddha's lap. Or maybe none of that was the case and they'd just happened to pinpoint my location on the exact night that Lance had made contact. Unlikely, but possible. In any case, even the dumbest human bounty hunter would have known enough to at least get a scalp or an eyeball for DNA confirmation of the kill. Thorson's dull-witted contraptions had left ground zero without so much as raking through the coals for my teeth.

My training always had me evaluating the enemy for a weakness. Unless I was missing something here, Thorson's reliance on technology over good ol' primitive human instincts and ingenuity qualified as a tactic that could someday turn around and bite him on the ass.

Not that it mattered to me anymore. It looked like I'd just been granted a free pass out of the shit parade. Both sides believed me dead. As far as anyone who mattered was concerned, I was no more. That came with a sense of freedom that I'd never known. I felt like a phantom lurking in a parallel world. I was on my own secret journey. This must be how the Abominable Snowman spends his time, I thought. And Sasquatch. Suddenly I was one of them – a free-ranging mythological beast.

I entertained this naïve way of thinking for almost one whole minute before I sobered up.

Maybe it was just my penchant for paranoia, but something felt off in my wishful thinking. Something I could almost taste on the frosty air. My instincts were telling me to watch my back.

The winter night was nearly over, and the faint glow of dawn was creeping along the jagged eastern horizon. I peered into the sky overhead. If you waited a moment, you'd spot one of the thousands of satellites moving in orbit around the earth. Sure enough – one came zipping through the stars. They always struck me as the worst sort of pollution – space-age intrusions in an otherwise pristine natural universe. I mean, who decided it was okay to desecrate this airy expanse of real estate so common to us all? Those spawn of Sputnik were symbolic of the secret technologies taking over our lives. They were Big Brother watching down on us, aka Björn-the-Omnipotent-Thorson. Not benevolently, with our wellbeing in mind, but monitoring the world for those of us threatening to throw a monkey wrench into the works of his machine.

Yeah, even a Yeti had to be watching over his shoulder these days.

That's what I reminded myself of as I set off across the mountains with my so-called freedom.

Rule number one, Bear Claw — Never second guess a maniac.

12

Lance

Recourse Plan F7 had been constructed from paradoxical logic.

In one regard, its aim was to bring me home without being discovered by Thorson's surveillance forces or some freelance bounty hunter hoping to collect a reward for my capture and delivery. Simultaneously, the plan was designed to lead all threats away from Colonel Cramer's center of operations. For all practical purposes, those two contradictory objectives cancelled each other out.

For several days, I trekked south out of Tibet and into Nepal.

Although I had no proof, I had to assume that the enemy was tracking my movements. At the same time, I needed to proceed as if I thought myself yet to be discovered, going "black," moving cautiously, both to make them believe I was leading them to their target if they were watching me, and also to actually evade detection if, in fact, they had yet to determine my position on the globe. Of course, I had no way of knowing under which set of circumstances I was working. The frustrating possibility was that I might be troubling myself with a problem that did not even exist.

And yet, I dared not take a chance and simply return directly to our secret headquarters. That could put my friends in danger. Not to mention that the fate of the world was at stake. If Thorson discovered Colonel Cramer and his allies, all would be lost. Those two factors took precedence over my personal desire to be back in the presence of my love interest.

"Moxie."

I voiced her name to the sky.

In truth, for me personally, she was the dominant factor in the equation, the overriding reason I was taking such pains and was so willing to put myself in danger. I was the unsung agent in her personal agenda.

Even though she didn't know it.

Moxie wanted revenge on Björn Thorson, and I was determined to help her get it. Thorson had had her manufactured as a plaything with the IQ of an eight-year-old girl. In addition, he had programmed her with a biblical devotion to no one but him. He had owned her in every sense of the word – in mind, body, and spirit. But since being damaged and subsequently repaired, Moxie had broken free of her mental slavery. Likewise, she had shed her naiveté like an outworn negligée. She was her own person now – reborn – complete with her own tastes, desires, and philosophies.

As well as her own psychological baggage.

An unfortunate byproduct in the evolution of becoming human.

Björn Thorson had been the catalyst for Moxie's process of individuation. He had also become the target for her submerged resentment – the one upon whom she had transferred all of her hatred and fury. He was the devil lurking in her shadow – an externalization of her internalized dark side that needed to be fought and subdued.

Moxie and her former owner were in a psychosomatic entanglement.

There is no way to convince someone mired in that mindset to be careful. They become myopic with their sense of justice. I knew this from my own experience. At one time, before she was murdered by Thorson's laser rays, my dear friend Eo had tried to guide me to a more measured approach when I had harbored the same feelings that were now tormenting Moxie. But although I had paid lip service to Eo's warnings, disguising my agenda as nothing more than an eagerness to learn about humans, I had secretly been developing my plans for vengeance against humanity as a whole, and Charlie Bear Claw in particular. A conflict I had been lucky to survive. Now, as I observed Moxie, I recognized the same process going on in her actions and speech. Beneath her placid façade simmered a recognizable rage.

And I needed to protect her from its negative consequences.

Björn Thorson was not a force to be taken lightly. A more merciless beast had never before stalked the planet. As Eo had been my guardian angel, so would I now be for Moxie. But unlike Eo, I had no intention of talking Moxie out of her vendetta.

Björn Thorson needed to be destroyed.

Yes, in order to save the world, of course. I would do all I could to facilitate that. But also to avenge Eo's death.

And yet, more importantly, Thorson needed to be eliminated so that he would no longer be a distraction to Moxie.

Only once the oppressor was reduced to smithereens could Moxie redirect her energies on falling in love with me.

13

Charlie

Traveling at elevation was pretty brutal for an out-of-shape, one-handed, navel-gazing passivist. It was basically winter alpinism without the safety of ropes, crampons, and the glorious objective of reaching a summit. I waded across the snowy slopes and ridgelines. I clung to the windswept rocks and ice. At night, completely spent, I burrowed into the drifts, curling myself into the fetal position and shivering in a restless half-coma until dawn.

Only to dig out in the morning, groggy and frostbit, to do it all over again.

I had no idea if it was worth all the trouble I was going through. Or all the suffering. Chances were good that no one was actually chasing me in the ways I imagined. Paranoia will destroy ya. And yet, I couldn't overcome my instincts. Back in my glory days of working covertly behind enemy lines, I took no chances. I did whatever I could to stack the odds in my favor. No matter how miserable it was, I did everything it took to survive.

Of course, a few things had changed since then.

In the old days, I had a focused sense of purpose – track down and terminate renegade robots. I was on a righteous crusade. I was a militarized zealot on a God-blessed crusade to rid the world of the evil unleashed by mankind's technological malfunctions.

Which is to say, I was screwy in the head – a brainwashed automaton driven by blind patriotism and a religious sense of honor.

It wasn't until later, long after both my wife and brother were dead, that I started to see things clearly. I'd only wanted to win approval from my so-called superiors. I wanted validation of my worth as a red man in the white man's world. Nothing made me feel more legit than having them tell me I was a great hunter. I was like a simpleminded hound who'd jump through any hoop he could just to get one of his master's belly rubs.

But that era was long gone. Now I was a devout practitioner of Wu Wei. My only mission was to stay alive, and even that was optional. But if I was ever going to achieve that goal, I'd have to deviate from my current tactics.

Step number one in that deviation would be to climb down off my mountain and rustle up some grub.

———

A finger ridge rose out of the canyon to where it leveled off onto a snowless acre before it turned steep again and swept back up to the snowy ramps from where I'd just come. Three kids were kicking a ball back and forth on the flat amidst a dozen grazing yaks. I crouched behind some rocks and scoped out the scene.

Between me and the pasture stood a stone building – a

sort of cowboy-style line-shack where the herders could get out of the weather. A string of red, green, and yellow prayer flags hung limply along the eave, and a whiff of lazy smoke twisted out of the chimney. Thumps, laughter, and the clang of yak bells echoed over the hillside.

Perfect, I thought. Get in, get food, and get out.

The door to the shack was on the opposite side from the pasture and I snuck inside unnoticed. A pair of steamy windows allowed daylight into the room's dim interior. Colorful rugs covered the dirt floor. A stack of milking pails. Sleeping mats. Some shelves loaded with blankets and ropes and harnesses. A pot and kettle sat steaming on the stove. The warm room smelled of burning yak dung and simmering soup.

My mouth watered.

I hadn't eaten in days.

The soup's what I wanted, but I didn't have time for a leisurely meal. I needed to grab something I could carry and then make like a yeti and vanish before the owners came home. Stepping over to the shelves, I dug around. I found a pair of walnut-sized potatoes and stuffed them into my pocket. Then I came across a plate of butter. I couldn't resist. I clawed into it and shoved the glob into my mouth. My whole body did a happy little dance as the rancid fat hit my tastebuds.

Oh, boy!

I sucked my greasy fingers and continued my hunt for food.

But all I found was some spices, a box of salt, and a few dry lentils in the bottom of a paper sack.

"Dammit!"

I emptied the sack into my mouth, crunching the lentils

between my teeth and turning them to sawdust.

Surely these people had more to eat than this. I searched some more, and then I reconsidered trying the soup. When I turned back toward the stove, the kids were coming through the door.

A boy, a girl, and another boy.

All of them about twelve or thirteen years old.

One of the boys was carrying a pail of milk. The other had a soccer ball under one arm. They were dressed in a mix of traditional and modern clothes – patched jeans, yak hair jackets, and sneakers. The girl was wearing a flannel skirt over her jeans.

To say the least, I felt awkward. And a little sheepish. It had to be obvious what I'd been up to. I wiped the butter off my chin, gave them a little bow, and smiled.

"*Tashi delek,*" I said. Hello.

The girl bowed to me. "*Tashi delek.*"

Then we just stared at one another for a minute, with me grinning like a boob.

At last, they all three came on into the room and went about their business as if my presence was perfectly normal. The girl started speaking to me. I had gotten semi-fluent in Tibetan, but I was only catching a little of what she was saying. I'd been traveling south for days, and chances were that I'd crossed the border into Nepal without knowing it. She was speaking another dialect. Maybe they were Sherpa. Her tone was friendly. When words failed us, she gestured for me to take off my coat and sit.

I knelt on the rug while she stoked the fire in the stove.

The boy with the milk pail went to the shelf, filled a blue bowl, and handed it to me.

I thanked him, "*Lolo ouskham,*" and peered into the bowl.

The milk was covered with foam and was still warm from the animal it had just been drawn from. I nodded gratefully to the boy and tipped the bowl into my mouth. With eyes closed, I gulped and gulped it down, the milk's power coursing through my withered body. I felt as if I were kneeling at the very teat of the Cosmos.

When I was finished, I licked the foam from my upper lip and burped.

The boys laughed.

So did I.

Next, the girl filled my bowl with hot soup. Milk broth with barley, curds, and potatoes. I had never tasted anything so good.

After I'd eaten my fill, the girl poured out four tin cups of black butter tea, and we all kneeled in a circle, nodding to one another while sipping our hot drinks. The boys were so handsome. The girl so pretty. Their cheeks were rosy from the chill air of the high mountains. The boys' black hair stuck out every which way, as if a yak had licked their heads, but the girl wore her hair in neat braids bound with red ribbons and beads.

I was admiring them, enjoying their soft conversation, when it hit me.

Holy cow!

The boys were twins!

I don't know. Maybe I was just punchy from my ordeal. Or blame it on altitude sickness. I'd have been hard-pressed to explain what came over me at being in the presence of those three sweet, beautiful kids. I felt myself swept away on a breaking flood of dammed-up emotion.

A real mix of happiness and grief.

A lump the size of a boot settled in my throat.

And then big hot tears started rolling down my cheeks.

14

I cried like a heartbroke sissy.

The tears just kept coming.

The sobs.

The girl came over and put her hand on my arm, speaking gently. I had no idea what she was saying, but the tone of her voice made me think of my mom.

Then the boys started singing. A real pretty tune that filled me up with warmth. It was like being in a private church.

Or in a forest with birds.

It was like having the Great Mother Bear hold you close while angels gave you comfort.

———

Once I was all cried out, I wiped my face with my hand and smiled apologetically to my hosts. They were understanding. They didn't embarrass me for my weepy little outburst. Instead, they showed me sympathy and respect. Their reaction carried all the best qualities of being human. It was nice to know that such a warm-hearted sentiment could still survive in this cold-hearted world.

I wanted nothing more right then but to stay with those kids. They could have been youthful reincarnations of me, my wife Shadow, and my twin brother Cody. Clear over here on the opposite side of the world from our Rocky Mountain birthplace. If I hadn't been such a resolute atheist, I would have said God was messing with me, tempting me with this perfect fairytale paradise for some reason I couldn't yet understand. I ached to live with these kids in their mountains with their animals and learn their language and be with them under their big Himalayan sky. A sort of pastoral replay of my own youth, one where I could change all the things I'd done wrong the first time around.

But I couldn't.

It was too risky.

There was no way I could take the chance of having the same thing happen to them that had happened to Dawa and his buddies.

Instead, I thanked the kids for their hospitality and stood. *"Lolo ouskham."*

They stood too, the girl speaking to me. I could tell she was asking me to stay. She opened her arms to the room, as if telling me to make myself at home.

"Thanks," I said, "but I can't."

As I slipped into my coat and moved toward the door, the girl said something to the boys and they both hurried across the room, one of them sliding a wooden lid from a stone crock in the corner, while the other pulled a yak skin blanket from the shelf. The boy at the crock held up a package in wax paper and said, *"Chhurpi."*

Hard cheese.

Then he went to his brother and rolled the package into the yak skin, binding it at both ends with a leather strap. They presented it to me as a gift and I looped the strap over my shoulder so that the roll hung on my hip under my arm without a hand. Then they followed me outside where I thanked them one more time before I walked away.

I could feel their gaze on my back as I started up the trail, but looking back would have been dangerous. I didn't think I'd be strong enough to resist the tractor beam of their Sherpa hospitality. I'd have been sucked back into their cozy shack.

"Don't do it, Bear Claw," I muttered. "Just keep walking."

I repeated those lines a hundred times, until I'd climbed back up to the snow.

15

Lance

Dead yaks half-buried in mud.

Thousand-year-old villages reduced to rubble.

Soiled prayer flags tangled in landslide debris.

I was met with these disturbing scenes a number of times as I traversed the Himalayas.

The glaciers in the mountains were shrinking at an alarming rate due to human caused climate change. The milky blue meltwaters gushed down the slopes into the lakes, swelling them beyond capacity, until they burst through the terminal moraines serving as their natural dams. Any human habitation downstream would be destroyed in the resultant flood, its inhabitants either killed or displaced, downgrading this once bucolic paradise to a hell on earth.

Björn Thorson, and the billionaire one percent of the population he counted as his sycophants, were the only ones powerful enough to reverse the cataclysmic course of events. They had become the only societal force with enough wherewithal and authority to stop the catastrophe. And yet, the climate tragedies playing out across the globe did not directly touch them. By means of their vast wealth, this elite group was able to remove itself from the fate suffered by their fellow Homo sapiens, as well as the countless other species of plants, insects, and animals falling victim to climate-related extinction with every passing day. The ultra-wealthy enclave remained immune and indifferent, more concerned with preserving their privileged status at the top of the hierarchical food chain than helping those less fortunate. In fact, many of their group had actually reached their lofty positions by directly contributing to the earth's environmental degradation through oil production, mining, land development, and the manufacture of plastics and toxic chemicals.

As an intelligent nonbiological being without the same basic survival requirements of a human, I was able to observe the unfolding disaster objectively. The problem as I witnessed it was that the mass of humanity had become dependent upon, if not addicted to, the very goods, ideals, and services with which their overlords were controlling them. Although there were less destructive alternatives to those products, and to the dogmas driving their use, those in power had no intention of exploring those options and risk losing their control. Therefore, inadvertently, through the insatiable consumption of those goods, and through the opioidal advertising and religious propaganda conditioning the public into believing that this was the only way for them to live and prosper, the general population had been fueling the very machine that was now eating them alive.

Although the public's general apathy, gullibility, and inaction had initially played a part in their own destruction, a growing defiance had since been born as people began to realize the devastation wrought by the paradigm under which they were being manipulated. Unfortunately, by the time this defiance had taken hold, it was largely too late for anyone to successfully fight back. The once failsafe democratic institutions had broken down as those in control undermined the governing methodologies through misinformation. Sham leaders were securely ensconced and could no longer simply be voted out of office. Thorson and his puppet dictators and oligarchs had either bought any opposing governments and militaries with their bribes and corruption, or they had destroyed them with their weapons. Even the most diplomatically skilled and conscientious countries had proven ineffective against Thorson's technological methods for suppression.

That only left the guerilla factions of ecowarriors.

Of which Colonel Cramer's team was one of the last rebel holdouts.

It had been nineteen days since my final communication with their headquarters. I could not even be sure that they had not since been eliminated by Thorson's most effective means of crushing the resistance.

I was traveling in the shadow of Ama Dablam when that doomsday tool appeared above the great peak's summit. A large black Z – Thorson's emblem – was printed on its shell like a reworked Swastika. The silver orb patrolled the skies, drifting quietly as a cloud, its all-seeing eye sweeping the landscape for any pockets of rebellion.

That Orwellian sky ship was now the world's most ruthless hunter.

And we, the resistance, were its prey.

It was Thorson's deadliest high-tech predator to date –

The Pyrotomic Obliterator.

16

Charlie

The yak skin was a major upgrade to my survival kit. After a long day of tramping over the heights, I'd scoop out a hole in the wind-crusted snow, crawl inside, wrap up in my wooly blanket, melt a lump of ice on my tongue, and nibble on some hard salty cheese.

The lap of primitive luxury.

Once I was fed, reasonably warm, and without much to do until dawn, I kicked back and enjoyed a little me time.

The mountains slept.

While the earth twirled through space.

"What topic shall we discuss this evening, Charlie?"

Yeah, I'll admit it. I talked to myself quite a bit on those long winter nights, teetering on my tightrope of sanity. Thin air and solitude will do that to you. Along with crushing fatigue.

I rubbed my stump – my new nervous habit – reliving that moment when I cut off my hand. The regular memories – blood, pain, and the shockwave shooting through my body as I jumped from the plane.

"Would you do it again, Bear Claw, if you could go back?"

"Good question, Self. Let me think about it."

At the time, I hadn't realized all the pieces of my predicament. I believed I was in more danger than I actually was, most likely being delivered to Thorson's lair for a torture party and a fun-filled game of twenty questions. Now I understood that Moxie was probably just transporting me and Lance to Cramer's headquarters.

Oops!

Who knew?

But in that moment, chained as I was to the robot, I'd felt confused and desperate, like an animal in a trap. I was willing to chew off my own paw to get free. Or, as it turned out, I was willing to chop off my own hand with a titanium tomahawk. It had been a spontaneous move, and without much thought behind it. An instinctual act of self-preservation by a noble savage.

I shifted in my yak skin with a sigh. Hmm. Something felt a little wonky in that rationale.

"The truth, Charlie. What's the actual truth?"

I really hated the truth.

The truth, if I were being an honest Injun, was that I had wanted to take myself out of the game. I was suddenly sick of the fighting and the killing and the torment those two activities were inflicting on my life. I wanted to be rid of the hand that had killed my wife. I wanted the torture to stop. I wanted some peace.

"There," I said. "That's the truth."

On that fateful day on the Chameleon Hawk, something in me had decided that a warrior with only one hand could no longer be a warrior. It might have come across as a selfless act, as if I were sacrificing my own wellbeing for someone else, but that was really just a misinterpretation. Lance had misread my gesture. Dumb robot. He thought I'd somehow done it to spare him. He'd led himself to believe that I had mutilated myself in order to promote the cause of his love for Moxie. But that wasn't right. I'm not that nice of a guy. In reality, I was just like one of those soldiers who shoots himself in the foot in hopes of getting pulled from the horror of the battlefield. Only I'd done a much better job of fooling everybody of my true intentions.

Heck, for a while afterward, I'd even fooled myself. But I could no longer hide from the troubling truth. It hassled me every night with its procession of ghosts and doubts.

So would I do it again if I could? A worthless question. What's done is done. Hands don't grow back. There are no do-overs in this shitshow.

For anything.

I'd come to accept that as a cold hard fact.

No matter how much I might try to rewrite the past, avoid reality, or pay for my sins and stupidity, regret was now my way of life.

And it didn't look like there was a damn thing I could do that was ever going to change that.

17

Lance

My aural intake regulators were dialed to their widest range of frequency gathering capabilities in order to detect any incoming kill devices intended for my termination. Therefore, I was able to pick up the high-pitched whine of the Pyrotomic Obliterator's thermostatic regulators and anti-gravitational boosters before it moved into position over the deep valley at the foot of Ama Dablam.

An unsettling reverberation shook the air, like the purr of a mechanized beast.

At roughly one kilometer from where I was watching, there stood a two-story stone and clay stucco building. A herd of yaks was grazing on the unseasonably snowless slope immediately below it, while a swollen glacier-fed river twisted and rushed down the valley. Rarified sunshine illuminated the overall landscape.

Until the scene was eclipsed by the Obliterator's cold shadow.

The colossal spheroid hovered weightlessly over the drainage, rotating slowly, sadistic in its mien.

Soon after, as the people below became aware of the danger, a bell began to clang, and the building's inhabitants poured from its doors. The shouts and calls of frantic men, women, and children echoed over the hillside.

A man and woman, each armed with shoulder-mounted rocket launchers, knelt side-by-side on the building's roof. They fired their anti-aircraft weapons simultaneously, the projectiles blazing a smoking path toward the threat over their heads. But the rockets exploded short of their target as they slammed into the layer of impenetrable energy comprising the Obliterator's invisible forcefield.

Others in the rebel group fired rifles at the orb, the pops of their antiquated weapons sounding decidedly quaint in light of the technological monstrosity toward which their tiny bullets were directed.

A defiant gesture.

About as effective as throwing marbles at an elephant.

Ultimately, a gleaming black barrel telescoped from a retractable panel below the orb's eye. It rotated at an angle, adjusting its coordinates, and then, nonchalantly, it fired.

A beam of blurred sub-matter, its particulates focused in a thermonuclear transmission of quark fusion, instantaneously power-zapped the building and its immediate environs.

A fiery flash ensued.

Followed by a crackle of disrupted molecules.

Leaving nothing in its wake but a smoking void on the hillside, and, theoretically, the wispy souls of yaks and ecowarriors disseminating over the lofty peaks.

18

Charlie

Something was wrong.

As I post-holed across that slope in the final hour of the day.

My grandfather's voice kept hissing in my ear, trying to warn me.

Dammit, Charlie, watch what you're doing!

But I must have been too lazy to listen. Or too tired to care.

Instead, head down, breathing hard, and sweating like a pig, I just kept tromping along. I was dead set on getting in as many miles as I could before dark, determined to cover some serious ground, until…

Whoomp!

That got my attention.

That deep down fracture.

I stopped. Tensed. And for the first time in hours, did an ad hoc hazards assessment.

The afternoon had been warm. Freakishly so for this elevation and time of year. If I had been paying attention to my environment, I would have noticed the snow decomposing under the heat of the sun, settling heavily on the mountainside, and turning to slush in my boot prints.

I lifted my gaze to the glistening seracs hanging over the cliffs in the evening alpenglow. Water spilled off the ice, washed into a crevasse, and then spread into a web of streamlets hidden under the snowfield. I was smack dab in the middle of the slope.

"Phooey," I mumbled. "This ain't good."

That's all it took.

The weight of my words.

There was a crack like pistol shot.

Next thing I knew, all hell broke loose.

Nothing in daily life really prepares you for a ride in an avalanche. Even a daily life like mine. I'd been ejected from flaming jets, stepped on by robots, and knocked flat by exploding bombs, but snowslides hold their own special kind of thrill.

The slope collapsed beneath my feet, triggering an adrenalin-flavored nausea. As I sank into the disintegrating snowpack, my instincts surged to full power. I needed to stay on top of the slide. I swam in the frosty tsunami, my arms beating as I swept along. That worked for a while, but then...
The undertow grabbed my heels and dragged me down.

As a roar filled my head.

I tumbled inside the violence. Somersaults and cartwheels. Wrenching my spine and popping my joints. The wave spit me to the top, letting me grab a breath, but then I plunged back down into the fluid white darkness.

I had no idea how long this ride was lasting. Seconds? Hours? Time's a different breed of animal when you're in the heat of the trauma.

At last, like a freight train hitting the brakes, everything screeched to halt.

My body stopped with a jolt.

As a moan escaped my throat.

Now came the fun part.

The ticking clock.

19

Immediately, I initiated the steps for avalanche survival.

Step number one – Don't panic!

Step number two – Thrash with every part of your body in order to enlarge the cavity where you're trapped. The reason? To make more space for air while you calmly wait for your friends to dig you out.

Only I was Charlie the friendless renegade.

I was flying solo.

No one in the whole world even knew where I was.

So, special case scenario survival step number three – Go back and redo step number one.

My eye sockets were packed with ice, but I managed to clear them off by batting my eyelids and wiggling my head. There was no visible light shining through any thin spots in the snow. Everything was black. A claustrophobic's nightmare. I felt like a shrink-wrapped steak at the forgotten bottom of a deep freeze. For all I knew, there could be twenty feet between me and the surface.

Not good.

Don't think about that.

Next step – Gather up a big wad of saliva and let it dribble out your lips. Gravity will pull it toward the center of the earth, telling you how you're oriented after your topsy-turvy trip down the mountain. That wasn't easy to do. I was suffering a severe case of cotton mouth. I worked and worked my jaws, wringing my tongue for moisture, until I finally gathered up a glob of spit and let it dribble out the corner of my mouth. A warm dampness trickled along my cheek, telling me that I was on my right side and up was to my left.

My right arm was twisted behind my back, while my left was positioned like I was waving. I half-heartedly pounded at the ceiling with my stump, but I had a limited range of motion, and the snow was setting up hard. The effort seemed like a waste of energy and air.

Not that I had any better ideas.

I was out of survival steps.

My oxygen supply was going fast.

It started to feel like a pillow was being pressed over my face.

Ways to escape, I thought. What are your options?

But there weren't any.

So… *Get ready for it, Bear Claw. Here it comes. After chasing you all these years, it's finally got you cornered.*

That hungriest of beasts.

Death.

———

Distantly, I heard a voice.

My mother's.

It was muffled, but I knew it was her.

I was hearing her from inside of her as she sang to me in Chompquaw.

Earth Bear holds her child in her arms.

Sky Bear waits for the dream to bring him home.

It was my earliest memory. From before I was even born. It had been resting inside of me my whole life, and now, in this oxygen-deprived fever dream, it was coming back from over the years.

My body shuddered.

Then relaxed.

Lullabies, I realized, are just funeral songs turned inside out. That had never dawned on me before. Birth and Death use the same door. One as an entrance, the other as an exit. That made me feel better. Although I couldn't have told you why. The asphyxiation was making it hard to think straight.

My breaths turned to shallow gasps. Almost spasms. I could hear my own heart.

And my mother's.

And then another heartbeat too.

That's when I realized I wasn't alone.

"Are you there?"

"Yes." He spoke to me in Bear. "I am with you."

It was a relief to have someone close.

"Dying," I asked. "Is it hard?"

"It's the easiest thing there is," he said. "But this is not your time."

That made me laugh.

"You must not go into the dream just yet. There is too much left to do."

I shifted in my icy womb.

"Earth needs *Idjmnukolpyumup* to be born again. The People of the Bear and those young people on the mountainside need you to fight."

"It's too late," I said. "Our time is over. The world is now run by autocratic monsters and their intelligent machines. Whatever will be, will be."

"No. You only need to wake the animal inside of you. The primitive force of *Katoyotapsommiki*."

I wanted that to be possible, but I felt doubt. "That part of me is extinct."

"No. It is only sleeping."

I wanted to believe him.

"That is why I am here," he said. "I have come to help you. Together we will dig you out of this darkness with our claws."

He started scratching at the packed snow on the ceiling.

"But all of our people are dead. Why can't I just quit fighting and be with you and them on the other side?"

"I am not dead. You must live for me."

He scratched again in the snow.

I was confused. "Cody?"

He continued to dig.

"Isn't that you, little brother?"

My eyes were adjusting to the dark. His shadow turned and looked at me and sighed.

"I am not your dead brother," he explained. "I am your someday son."

20

Everything after that was a blur.

Somewhere in the process, I must have switched on my auto-recovery skills and dug myself out.

When I finally snapped out of my hypoxic hallucination, I found myself on my knees panting next to a black hole in the runout zone of the avalanche.

Oh sure, I suppose you could try to convince me that my unborn son had rescued me, that I was delivered from the icy grip of death by some miracle or spirit. In a way, I suppose that's true. At the very least, the idea of him had inspired me enough to grow a pair and save myself. But to fully follow that way of thinking would mean rewriting the existential handbook for life I had been so painstakingly composing for the past few years. That would allow for God or a Great Mother Bear or even guardian angels, as well as opening the floodgates to a whole load of supernatural crapola I didn't have time to think about right now.

My current reality was a little too pressing for that.

Staggering to my feet, I squinted into the stars blinking on in the cold purple sky. I blew into my fingers and stomped the circulation back into my frost-numbed toes.

Although the day had been balmy, the descending night was a different story. The temps were already below zero and still dropping. I was soaked from wallowing in the snow. I'd lost my yak skin blanket in the slide. I needed to get moving before I turned into a Chompquaw-flavored popsicle.

After the first few steps, I stumbled and fell back to my knees. My body was one big bruise, my joints and tendons stretched like overworked bungee cords. It felt like my legs were on backwards. But no time to whine. I forced myself to my feet again and then settled into a painful pace of plunge-stepping down the snowy slope.

Once I reached the snowline, I started traversing the rocky hillside. My only plan at that point was to keep moving so that the ice wouldn't creep into my bones. Oddly, the farther I went, the stronger I felt. As if I were tapping into some sort of backup power reserve. It's hard to explain, but something inside of me was waking up and turning on.

I picked up my pace, hopping across the starlit boulder fields.

Still, there was no telling how long I could go before I ran out of gas. I needed shelter and rest. I needed a place to warm up.

And that's exactly when I caught a whiff of it.

Hanging there in the cold thin air.

I stopped short and lifted my face and drew a breath through my nose.

"It can't be," I said, almost laughing. "Unbelievable."

And yet it was true.

Although it was faint, that scent was unmistakable.

21

Lance

Something was wrong.

As I pressed through the bustling streets of Katmandu.

A warning signal had begun to quietly, but insistently, beep inside my head.

I struggled to maintain my composure as I entered the market district of the city.

Do not reveal your distress, I warned myself. *Appear calm.*

The clamor of human activity overwhelmed my auditory sensors, rendering them useless as a means of pinpointing the source of danger from within the sonic clutter. Which was probably irrelevant. Whoever was following me most likely had the technical competence to outwit my preemptive defense systems.

My purpose upon entering the city had been to shake any possible bounty hunters, human or otherwise, that might have picked up my trail in the mountains. That was an advised tactic embedded within Recourse Plan F7. It directed me to outmaneuver any possible threats by mingling with the milling crowds. Instead, it appeared, I had placed myself squarely in their sights.

The streets were lined with stalls from which merchants

were earnestly hawking their wares. Bolts of cloth, brass prayer bells, books, cell phones, loaves of naan, and statuettes of both Buddhist and Hindu deities.

I stopped before an old woman sitting cross-legged on the curb behind a basket of dried apricots. She was as wrinkled as the withered fruit she was offering to the passersby. The woman spoke to me, holding up a shriveled apricot in her bony palm, urging me to taste it.

I managed a smile for her while training my peripheral vision on the next stall. The corner post was adorned with mirrors. Obliquely, I scanned the images in the reflective ovals and squares until I found the one most relevant to my current dilemma.

A figure, subtly different from the others, was standing with its back to me on the opposite side of the street.

I performed an ad hoc character analysis based on the few visual clues I could gather.

Male. Moving with the pretense of indifference. Dressed in clothes designed for freedom of movement. The telltale bulge of a weapon tucked inside his jacket at the small of his back.

In short, an assassin.

In my anxiety, I had inadvertently let my full gaze fall on the mirror in which he was reflected, thus exposing my expression to him when he glanced my direction. Although I immediately turned away, our eyes had locked in the mirror for one-fifth of a second – long enough for him to recognize that I understood his intentions.

The chase was on.

22

Turning casually on my heel, I strolled away from the old woman with the apricots.

Through the congested street.

Around the corner.

To a row of rattletrap motorbikes parked along the curb.

Upon summarily assessing the machines, I chose the one that appeared to be in the best condition. I straddled the seat and kicked the starter. The internal combustion engine coughed smoke and clattered to life.

Jamming the bike into gear, I sped away.

My hope was to outrun my assailant before he ever rounded the corner. I felt optimistic about my chances until a particle wave whizzed past my ear and exploded into the side of a truck crossing the intersection before me.

I veered right.

The hunter had acquired a motorbike as well. Apparently, a better machine than mine. Although I was running my mount at full throttle, he was rapidly closing the distance between us.

I raced through the streets, weaving among the cars, their drivers leaning on their horns in protest of my recklessness.

Another particle beam grazed my right arm.

I swerved left.

Directly into oncoming traffic.

To avoid collision, I jumped the curb and motored down the sidewalk. Panicked pedestrians leapt from my path.

Until my motorbike died.

It just quit.

I dismounted while it was still rolling and stumbled into a somersault. The shoulder strap on my backpack snapped. The load shifted and drooped to one side as I scrambled back to my feet and whirled away from the approaching hunter. With his weapon raised over his handlebars, he fired.

The beam struck my backpack, blowing it apart and knocking me to the pavement.

I shed the smoking pack, lunged into an alley, and fled on foot.

The hunter's motorbike squealed to a halt.

As I ran, I visualized the hunter at the entrance to the alley dropping to one knee behind me...leveling his firearm... aligning its sights on the space between my shoulder blades... and then, just as he squeezed the trigger – *Zzzzzt!* – I dove through a side gate.

Into an enclosed courtyard.

A single yellow door hung on the far wall, and I dashed toward it. I tugged on the handle, but it didn't give. I tugged more forcefully. To no avail. I turned back to the yard, assessing the scene for possible routes of escape.

There were no other doors available. A rickety drainpipe ran up the adjoining corner, but it did not appear to be sturdy enough to support my weight in a climb. A number of windows opened onto the yard, but they were all out of reach from the ground. Some electrical wires drooped above, loaded with a flock of nervously cooing pigeons. The buildings towered on three sides of the enclosure, with the fourth side – the side with the gate – bordered by a tall sheet metal fence.

A weapon would have been helpful in this situation, but mine was in the pack that I had abandoned on the sidewalk.

With my back to the yellow door, I eyed the gate across the narrow yard, waiting for the enemy.

By all appearances, I was trapped.

———

Reflexively, I redirected my thought stream away from my current predicament to recollections of Moxie. If these were to be my last moments of awareness, I wanted to be enjoying her company, if only in my digitized imagination.

I power-scanned my memory banks for a replay of our first encounter. I liked to return to that recall whenever I could. I enjoyed remembering Moxie's smile on that sunny afternoon. I thrilled at the pleasing resonance of her laughter. Most poignantly, I relished our shared innocence of that time before we had gained enough knowledge to understand the difficulties of life.

So much had seemed possible on that day.

And so much had changed in the interim.

———

The hunter kicked through the gate and sprang into the yard, leading with his particle wave pistol. When he saw that I was unarmed, he relaxed his bearing.

I raised my fists in an attitude of self-defense.

Which made him grin.

There truly is a no more sadistic creature on the planet than a predatory human closing in on its helpless prey.

"Shall we discuss options?" I asked.

He laughed.

I felt like a sex toy of limited intelligence for allowing myself to get in this situation. I was a much better warrior than this. I knew that I was. But it appeared I would have no chance to transcend my baseline amorous programming and prove myself a hero.

The hunter stepped my way, his weapon held at waist level, like a gunfighter in an old western movie.

"I have important information which may increase my value if I were to be delivered intact," I said.

Of course, I had set my files to auto-scrub in the event of the sudden cessation of my life functions. There was no way I would divulge one byte of intelligence to the enemy, but I thought a bluff might work on this particular specimen and gain me some time. He did not appear to be of the highest caliber of his profession. He was rough, exhibiting the air of a second-rate thug. The man was likely working on his own, hoping to collect a bounty he had found advertised on the dark web, with no direct connection to Thorson himself.

The hunter stepped to within two meters of me and stopped.

"I am only saying that you could stand to gather a much bigger reward for my live capture than from my inanimate remains."

He did not appear to be buying my subterfuge.

Instead, he raised his weapon so that it was trained on my chest.

This appeared to be my final moment of awareness.

"Moxie." I whispered her name that one last time. "My love."

"Kiss your ass goodbye," growled the hunter.

I braced for termination.

But then the man's head exploded.

23

Charlie

I peeled off my wet clothes and boots and rolled everything up in my coat, tying it tight with the sleeves. Then I stood naked and shivering under the icy stars, studying the short cliff before me. The wall had been completely buried earlier in the winter, but now, after the recent spell of warm weather, the snow had melted back to a deteriorating drift, exposing the shallow opening at the base of the rock.

I drew a deep breath.

Muttered, *"Katoyotapsomikki."*

And dropped to my belly on the frozen dirt.

Pushing my bundle ahead of me, I wiggled into the hole.

———————

The sweet stench inside was familiar. Heck, if I'm being honest, it was downright inviting.

Bears, it turns out, are like people. It doesn't matter if they're rich or poor or whatever color, they smell the same all over the world. I had known Yellowstone Grizzlies like they were family members, but now I learned that Himalayan Brown Bears smell like family too.

My eyes adjusted to the near darkness as I squirmed into the open room of the cave. It was sizable for a den. Made cozy and warm with central heating – aka body heat.

The big sow's mass lay in a shadowy heap on the floor.

Her breaths came quiet in the dead air. Slow and far apart. And mixing with the sound of mewing and suckling.

I crawled closer, until I could see the pair of tiny cubs nursing off their hibernating mama.

———

At that moment, I couldn't be sure if this was really happening. I suspected maybe I was still back in the avalanche, and this was some sort of vision being granted to me at the threshold of death. Everything about it seemed meaningful and otherworldly. More felt than understood. Like a muddy poem. Or one of those old legends my grandad used to tell me, Cody, and Shadow while sitting around the campfire.

Whatever it was, I was grateful to have it.

I didn't want to scare it away.

Carefully, I unrolled my coat and quietly spread my clothes out on the rocks so they could dry.

Yawning, I stretched my back and legs. That avalanche had really done a number on me. I was one beat up redskin. I waited for the cubs to finish their meal, and then I snuggled up with them next to their mother for some good deep rest.

Wild sounds came to me from far away.

The echoes of owls.

The love songs of wolves.
And the timeless music of twirling planets.
I dreamed of my brother.
I dreamed of my son.

24

Lance

The bounty hunter's headless body swayed before me for a full 2.7 seconds…

And then flumped to the ground.

Stunned, I stared down at his lifeless remains, unsure of what had just transpired.

I scanned the sky. I scanned the yard and the tops of the surrounding buildings.

And then I saw the masked figure standing in one of the high windows. By the curvilinear outline of the figure's form, I deduced that it was female. She wore a full body suit designed to hide her heat signature from overhead surveillance. After shouldering her arc-ray sniper's rifle, she peered down at me.

An instant of positively charged energy passed between us. An abstract and intimate connection of silent communication.

I wordlessly thanked her for saving my life.

A flock of pigeons passed in the sky.

And then, with a nod of her head, she turned and disappeared.

25

Charlie

In killing my wife, I had also killed the unborn baby inside of her.

My child.

Our cub.

And the last member in the lineage of the People of the Bear.

I'd been pretty bold about confronting all the other hard issues during my ongoing self-therapy sessions. I had stared down some real monsters back at the monastery. But my kid was the one issue I'd kept buried deep inside. I knew it was there. I could feel it scratching with its claws. But I couldn't bear to dig it out and face it.

The guilt was just too much for me.

But it turns out that a man's big bad issues don't just go away. They're as patient as time. They're just waiting until you're at your weakest moment.

And then they pounce.

And yet, it didn't look like it was here to finish me off. No. Just the opposite. If anything, that tiny soul in Shadow's womb had turned out to be my salvation.

Earth needs Idjmnukolpyumup to be born again, he had told

me. *You must live for me.*

That's what saved me. His encouragement. That's what snapped me out of my Wu Wei passivity and changed me back into a man of action.

Although that was arguably my moment of conversion, I'd been a little too preoccupied at the time to notice any revelatory lighting strike. But now that I had a minute to think it over, awareness was settling in. I started to feel the return of my self-worth. But smarter this time around. And not so stinking schizo.

Yeah. There was no doubt about it. Something was going on. Something way bigger than me and my puny ass problems. I was just a player in the clown show. A force was nudging me forward. Was it the ghost of my dead kid? The collective unconscious? God the Father? Or some as yet unclassified trick of science?

I didn't figure it much mattered. They were all starting to seem like one in the same. Or at least they were working together as some sort of team of cosmological superheroes.

Whatever the case, a switch had flipped inside of me. It had been a long time since Charlie Bear Claw felt this directed in his life.

The bear cubs licked my toes, yanking me out of my thoughts.

I grinned and whispered to the pair of fur balls rolling around in the shadows. "Hey, you rascals. Good morning."

My voice surprised me. It came out speaking Chompquaw. And with the same tone my grandfather always used with me and Cody when we were little kids.

Weak daylight leaked in through the cave's small entrance, faintly illuminating the details of the room. I scooped my hands into the loose sand on the floor. It was full of broken seashells – debris from when the Himalayas were thrust from the bottom of the ocean some fifty million years ago.

It kind of made a guy feel like nothing but a blip on the geologic timeline.

After that, I found a fire ring. As old as the last ice age. Think BCE. Bits of bones and antlers were scattered in the ashes – artifacts in this prehistoric time capsule. I pictured my primitive brothers and sisters sitting around the flames and singing songs to the mountains and sky, the flickering orange light casting their smoky shadows over the walls. I felt a kinship with them. I longed for that simpler time, back when mankind was young and people were connected to Nature, back when the term *modern technology* meant nothing more than shaping an arrowhead out of flint. I imagined myself as one of their clan. And then I tipped my gaze upward.

Vague figures appeared on the ceiling.

Like birds through thin clouds.

I dug the hologram projector out of my coat pocket and punched in the code. Overriding the imaging controls, I used the gizmo as a flashlight and aimed its beam at the cave's ceiling.

A thrill flushed through my body as the light washed over the stone.

Followed by a rush of goosebumps.

My mouth dropped open in awe as I stood with my light and examined the ceiling more closely. It was covered with drawings in red ochre. Many millennia old. All working together to tell some local rendition of the Big Picture. The phrase Stone Age Cinema came to mind.

Yaks with wings. Bears walking arm-in-arm with yetis. Cro-Magnon robots. Women and children and men dancing across a sky littered with planets and stars and what looked like ancient spaceships.

The cubs wrestled in the seashells at my feet as I studied the artwork.

Their snoozing mama sighed.

All of these pictures were fodder for the big sow's postpartum dreams. An interplay of reality and history and fairytales working into the mother bear's underthoughts as she dreamed the world further into its existence.

That made me laugh at myself. It wasn't my habit to get all mythological. I'd leave that to the preachers and medicine men of the world. Still, I was feeling more devout than I ever had in my life. More reverent and humble.

I explored the rest of the ceiling with my light. It was a prehistoric equivalent to the Sistine Chapel. Most of the paintings were over the center of the cave, but there was a lone figure away from the others, watching everyone from the back of the room. I stepped over and studied it more closely.

It made me smile.

Sure, I suppose it could have been inspired by some eternal deity or alien who had visited Earth from a distant world, but I figured it was more likely just the red ochre recall of a caveman's wet dream.

The woman in the image was tall and thin, her body covered in designs.

She had four eyes.

A knowing and pleasant smile.

And four breasts.

One pair above another.

26

The bear cubs nuzzled up to their mama for breakfast while I got dressed.

My head was churning with thoughts and questions. The biggest one being – what the hell should I do now?

Yes, my son had inspired me. But to do what?

Short answer – Save the world.

So okay, roger that.

But could I reasonably take on Björn Thorson by myself? Honestly, as much fun as that sounded, it didn't take a genius to see that it was a doomed strategy – a suicide mission resulting in nothing more than the grisly death of the world's last member of the Chompquaw Nation. I mean, for crying out loud, that maniac had at least a hundred different high-tech gadgets for sniffing me out and turning me into a grease spot. So no, that route was a dead end. To bring down this monster, I'd probably need some help.

"Rats, Bear Claw! You screwed up."

As much as I hated being in the company of robots, I was kicking myself now for not going with Lance. That had been my best chance, and I blew it.

Although I hadn't spotted any sign of it, there was still

a pretty good possibility that I was being tracked by the bad guys. Assuming that they actually knew I hadn't been killed in their raid on the monastery, they could have easily followed my trail when I headed off into the mountains without me ever knowing it. But even if my evasion tactics had been working, and I was still off their radar, how could I ever contact Cramer without blowing his cover and getting him killed? Not that I had any idea where he and his friends were hiding anyway.

I needed more intel.

To that end, I switched on my trusty hologram projector, turned down the volume, and replayed Cramer's message in the empty air at the back of the cave.

I played it through once, twice, three times, trying to hear the message beneath the message, the hints between the words in Cramer's voice that might tell me where he was when he recorded the broadcast.

"Planet Earth needs you," said Cramer. That line plunked a little harder in my head than the others.

Still, I wasn't getting anywhere, so I stopped the machine and studied the frozen instant where the colonel took off his glasses and cleaned them.

The man was good at playing hide and seek. Too good, I was beginning to think.

I sat cross-legged on the floor, rubbing my stump, thinking.

"*Yonkoy,*" I said, which is basically just Chompquaw for *Phooey.*

I glanced over to the bear family. The cubs had finished their breakfast and were snuggled down for another nap against the warm fur on their mother's belly. One cub had his arm thrown over his brother's shoulder.

"Living the good life."

Then I had an idea.

I played the message forward about four seconds, to the point where Cramer put his glasses on and turned back to the camera. I stopped it there. But this time, I used the zoom feature. Placing my hand in the airy image of the hologram, I spread my fingers, directing the focal point, enlarging the colonel's backdrop, and searching for clues in the steel wall behind him. Sometimes the military stamped the destination of the interlocking panels for shipment. I scanned every inch of the wall until I found some markings in the bottom corner. Of course, they'd been scratched out.

So I trained my attention on Cramer himself. Starting low, I zoomed in on his feet, searching for important information that might be revealed in his boot laces…his pant legs…his sweater…his hands…and finally, his face.

I tightened the image on his eyes. Then I tightened it again, until I picked up the faintest reflection in his glasses

"Yes!"

It took me a minute to manage the more complicated controls on the projector, but I managed to resolve the image and reduce the distortion, as well as increase the contrast, define the image, and dial back the shadows.

"Bingo!"

I sat back on my heels as Cramer's team lined up before me in the cave.

They were a motley crew.

And full of surprises.

27

Lance

Furtively, I proceeded through the environs of Katmandu and then on into the Nepalese southlands toward India. I still had no definitive evidence that my movements were being tracked. The incident with the bounty hunter had led to more questions than answers.

Foremost of these was – Who had saved me?

It was quite possible that it had been an asset sent by Björn Thorson himself. After all, if the bounty hunter had been successful in terminating me, I would no longer be able to lead the enemy to Colonel Cramer's secret base of operations. That rogue hunter obviously had not received the memo telling everyone to leave me alone. Therefore, an agent was sent to stop him.

That was the most feasible explanation for what had happened. It was also the wisest conclusion to incorporate into my ongoing process of problem solving. To allow for another account, one based more on wishful thinking than the clearheaded strategy of a fugitive, could very likely lead to the destruction of all my friends, myself, and the planet we were trying to save. I was no longer so naïve as to follow that tempting thought stream of fairytale optimism.

Nevertheless…

Something had passed between myself and the sniper as she peered down at me from the roof. Something vital. And intimate.

Of course, it had not been a scientifically measurable force. Not a mathematical interaction of quantifiable properties. Which eliminated it for consideration from a purely rational standpoint. And yet, I had traveled too far down the evolutionary path of my own developing humanity to completely dismiss it. For I well knew that many of an individual human's most pivotal decisions in life were prompted less by empirical evidence than by an intuitive and abstract sense of reality.

So no, I would not succumb to hopeful self-deception

At least not in the strictest sense of the concept.

But neither would I completely dismiss the positive emotion that had passed between myself and that lady sniper. It too strongly resembled the interplay of energy I had felt three years earlier when walking hand-in-hand on the moonlit dunes with Eo.

That had been the irrefutable force of Love.

It was highly improbable that a random sniper under orders from Thorson would transmit such a positive quantum pulsation in my direction. And so, I allowed that she had not come to my aid under orders from that megalomaniac, but had instead come of her own volition, from a different camp entirely, out of a fondness for me. A fondness that she had, for some reason beyond logic, felt disinclined to express when in my company.

Yes, this was all conjecture. I needed to stress that to myself. It was a thinly supported hypothesis driven largely by my deepest desires and logistically improbable. But I could not completely discount the possibility that if I were to pull the mask from that guardian angel, I might find none other than the face of my dear Moxie.

28

Charlie

I sat in the back of the cave and studied the holographic image of the folks reflected like ghosts in Cramer's glasses.

Front and center in the group was none other than Lance's servo-driven heartthrob Moxie. She was operating the camera for the colonel's monologue. She looked good. A real doll. But one who had ditched her bedroom plaything persona and replaced it with a big load of whup-ass G.I Jane spunk.

She wore the sneer of a rebel.

I liked that in a girl.

It occurred to me that Moxie might just be the only robot I'd ever thought worth the epoxy and rivets holding her together.

Standing at the she-bot's shoulder was – surprise, surprise – Judy Baxter.

This was starting to look like a reunion of Lance's girlfriends – the one he longed to be with next to the gorgeous dominatrix from his past.

I shook my head. "Why do the weirdos always get the hot girls?"

Ms. Baxter was looking really nice too. Healthy. She had cut her hair and was standing a little straighter than the last time I saw her. Her eyes were green and bright. No longer fogged with vodka. She wore fatigues with a knife on her belt. A departure from her usual miniskirts and tight sweaters.

I recalled the time back in Judy's apartment when she had leaned against my chest and kissed me, triggering an electric jolt that shot through every inch of my manhood. That struck me as one of the highlights in my pitiful recent life. A moment I liked to bring out and think about whenever I got a chance. Judy Baxter had hired me to hunt down and bring back Lance unharmed after his so-called malfunction. A job I had seriously botched.

Standing on the other side of Judy was my old pal Atu. That ecowarrior brought some serious battle cred to the mix. The man had been in the shit a hundred times and was still going strong.

Next up in the roll call – Dr. Capek, of Droidware Laboratories. He was the brainiac scientist behind the creation of Judy's Hollywood handsome bedfellow, aka Lance the cuddly mandroid. Capek wore his usual lab coat and worried expression. He was always chewing at the corner of his mustache.

After Capek came Brita Jónsdóttir. I had the pleasure of first meeting her when she kicked my butt in a scuffle back in Iceland. She left me with a nice big scar on my forehead and a badly battered ego. Like Atu, Brita was a force of nature. A real asset to the colonel's team.

There were a dozen other people in the room as well. Both male and female of all races. Technicians mostly. Nerds with slide rules. But a few military personnel as well, what I figured were Cramer's faithful guerillas brought over from AWOL Weapons Retention.

I studied this company of misfit rebels. What had brought them all together? Judy Baxter seemed especially out of place. The common objective of the group seemed to be battling Thorson in order stop his devious plans for the end of the world.

Yeah, it was a page torn right out of an action-packed comic book. Only with wannabe heroes who could bleed and break and be blown to smithereens by the evil one they were trying so hard to bring down. If you studied the odds, the smart money was on Thorson.

I wasn't finding any clues to tell me where they were, so I zoomed in even closer on their individual figures. Then I dialed in on the wall at the back of the room behind them. It took a lot to resolve the image so that it was readable, but I managed to tighten on a pair of monitors, one displaying a satellite image of Earth, and the other a series of coordinates on a map.

4°53'06"N53°41'28"E

I had no idea if the coordinates were significant, but I committed them to memory just in case. Chances were, they might lead me to Cramer's hideout. I just had to be sure I didn't lead Thorson to Cramer at the same time.

I felt like I had gleaned about all I could from the hologram, but I decided to scan it one more time just in case I'd missed something. Sure enough, there was a face in the crowd that I hadn't noticed. I tightened in on the man standing in the shadows and a little to the side.

"Jeepers!"

He was the biggest surprise of the bunch, and I'd nearly missed him.

I recognized the guy's face from the intel reports I had

studied years earlier while prepping for a mission that I'd really just like to forget. And yet, here he was again, just another living ghost from my troubled past.

Professor Rajat Peeples.

A biochemist of exceptional talents.

And the man who had discovered Deilonium.

29

Lance

The Uttar Pradesh region of northern India was geographically the opposite of the Himalayas. The low elevation plains were flat and well-populated. Instead of the melting glaciers of the high mountains, drought and wildfires were the dominant manifestations of global warming.

Apocalyptic smog hung over the landscape.

I traveled by public bus for some kilometers until the vehicle ran out of petrol and we passengers were forced to disembark. The infrastructures and economies of societies around the globe were failing at an exponential rate with the initiation of Thorson's first steps in planetary reengineering. Supply chains had broken, and the distribution platforms of basic commodities such as food and fuel had all but collapsed.

Phase one in Thorson's scheme allowed this socio-ecological travesty to play itself out without intervention.

As I continued down the dusty roads on foot, I encountered groups of climate refugees, all of them fleeing the fires that were consuming the sun-scorched grasslands and dying forests of their homeland.

Men, women, and children.

Hungry, parched, and exhausted.

Wearing the listless expressions of zombies, these displaced souls carried their worldly possessions in bundles, either balancing them on their heads, or dragging them in the dirt at their heels.

Due to the inorganic properties of my own physical composition, I was immune to the biotic disruptions facing these fragile members of the ecosystem. Indeed, I was entirely suited to the very conditions that were proving so detrimental to everyone else. Still, I could not help but feel a pang of sorrow upon regarding these carbon-based creatures in the midst of their plight.

It was puzzling how I, a nonhuman construct made of synthetic materials, could feel more sympathy for these reluctant nomads than did certain flesh and blood members of their own species. Specifically, it was incomprehensible how Björn Thorson and his well-off associates could so easily disregard the utter unraveling of the fabric of humanity while doing nothing to stop it. As the travesty played itself out around the world, those overlords enjoyed the privileged luxuries of self-proclaimed deities. While all other life on the planet faced extinction, due largely to the environmentally detrimental practices by which the elites had achieved their wealth, the Highborns kept themselves removed from the danger, entertaining themselves in the self-indulgent production of private rocket ships and building terraformed playgrounds on the moon, while somehow convincing themselves that their callousness and self-absorbed preoccupations were justified as evolutionary proof of the Darwinian principle of survival of the fittest.

And yet, they were still just humans, their status founded not so much on their superior strength or intellect, but on luck. Urinating in a gold-plated toilet might have marked them as privileged, but it did not allow them exemption from their own inevitable mortality.

Indeed, with our nondegradable parts and the new power source implemented by Dr. Capek and Professor Peeples, Moxie and I could easily outlast them all.

———————

Ultimately, I came to the Ganges River. Due to the melting glaciers and snowfields far upstream at its headwaters, the river was flooded, creating an ironic contrast to the drought-stricken land through which it flowed.

Fields lined the banks of the river, but the recent heat waves had taken a toll. Even though they were close to a source of irrigation, the twigs of failed crops poked hopelessly from the cracked and thirsty earth.

It was in the middle of one such barren field that I saw a scene that gave me pause.

A skinny Brahman cow stood in the hazy sunlight like a statue carved of calcium carbonate. But it was not so much the chalk-colored bovine that caught my attention, as the listless figure on the ground beside it.

I had witnessed many disheartening scenes in the recent weeks. Many travesties of famine and ecological devastation. Had I involved myself in the ever-present misery, my progress would have been brought to a standstill. I reminded myself that Colonel Cramer's plan for defeating Thorson took precedence over the problems of individuals. The common good of the entire human race and the planet on which it dwelled was more important than the troubles of any single member of the global community.

I needed to keep moving.

I needed to stay focused on my mission.

And yet, there was something in this woeful figure that pulled at me with the measurable force of a magnet.

I gazed down the road before me. There were many kilometers yet to travel, and time was running out, but I couldn't help myself. Over the span of my own brief existence, and through the trauma and heartache I myself had suffered in that time, I had inadvertently developed an exaggerated capacity for empathy.

There was no escaping it.

By all measurable indicators, I, Lance the android, had traveled one more irrevocable step toward being human.

Helpless to do otherwise, I quickly crossed the field to the pathetic figure cowering in the shadow of the cow.

30

Charlie

The coordinates in the hologram image were the only clue I had that might tell me where to find Cramer's hideout. Of course, they could just as soon lead me to a dead end. But I didn't have any better ideas, and if Cramer's message was true, my time was running out. I had to do something fast, so I got out the big world map I kept folded in my brain, dialed in those compass readings, and formed a plan of action.

It wouldn't be easy.

Not if Thorson was watching me.

I'd have to wing it as I went along. Leading that diabolic scumbag to the colonel would sort of defeat the purpose. Still, my first move was obvious.

I needed to get to the ocean.

———

Heading south, I slipped out of Nepal into India.

So long Buddhism, hello Hinduism.

Out of the enlightened embrace of Buddha and into the

multiple arms of Shiva.

Everything here ran on that underlying fairytale.

I get it. The world's a scary place. We're all quaking in our boots most of the time. Or weeping in our sleep. We're all of us all too human. You can't really blame folks for wanting something they can believe in, some ready-made system with an all-powerful protector watching over them to give them hope in the midst of their terrifying lives.

But the problem as I saw it was that the only one watching wasn't some benevolent deity, but the very devil himself – that fiend Thorson. Guys like him have been using the collective psychology of the masses for their own ends ever since Adam broke the rules and got his sinful ass kicked out of Eden. Every corner of the world has its own version of that same old scam. Superstitions were just ways for the lucky bastards on top to control the peons at the bottom.

Only now the stakes were greater than at any other time in history.

Thorson was about to take complete control of everything.

Meanwhile, here I was traveling through the land where the caste system had been woven into the fabric of daily life for thousands of years. Ask any untouchable if he thought he was getting a fair shake in this life and his brainwashed answer would no doubt be yes, and that he just needed to buck up, accept his sorry lot, and do every subservient thing he could for his superiors in order to improve his karma.

Pitiful.

But I wax cynical about my fellow idiots.

If I was ever going to help, I needed to stay focused on my mission.

The difficulty facing me right now was getting anywhere considering the state of the public transportation system.

Nothing was running. Airports were closed. There were no cars or buses on the roads, just haggard pedestrians. The trains stood idle on the tracks in the middle of the plains, abandoned in the place where they ran out of fuel. It was hot. Fires were burning in every direction, leaving the air heavy with smoke. The world had obviously been suffering a major downgrade while I was hiding out in Shangri La. Everything had gone to hell.

I traded my hiking boots for a knapsack and a pair of rubber sandals, and my parka for a rickety bicycle with wobbly wheels and a rusty chain.

Then I pedaled south towards Armageddon.

31

Lance

The girl sat beside the cow with her knees drawn up and her forehead resting on her folded arms. Her bare feet were burrowed into the dirt beneath her. Although her cotton dress was adorned with a pattern of colorful flowers, it was faded and threadbare and filthy. Based on her size, I calculated her to be six or seven years old.

"Namaste," I said.

At first, the girl didn't respond, and I thought perhaps she was sleeping, but then she slowly lifted her head and peered up into my face.

Her large brown eyes blinked against the somber sunlight.

I smiled and, speaking in Hindi, asked, "Are you alright?"

She regarded me as if not knowing how to answer such a ridiculous question. How, she asked wordlessly, could she, or anyone else for that matter, possibly be *alright*?

The cow chewed impassively with an empty mouth, her eyes half-closed, randomly swishing her tail at flies.

The girl and I assessed one another. She made no effort to speak. I noted the faded red dot on her forehead slightly above the middle of her eyebrows. Her tilaka mark, or third eye. Logically, I knew that it was nothing but a dab of red paint, no more than a token of her Hindu faith. And yet, it seemed as if that eye were peering directly into the mechanizations of my own robotic soul.

Some years earlier, as I first ventured into the world on my own, I had met a devout young man named Nephi Olsen. He became my first friend. Although I had since come to think of him as childishly naïve, at the time I believed Nephi to be the wisest person I knew. I often recalled our first meeting.

I accessed my memory banks and reviewed the transcript of the conversation in which Nephi told me about a concept he called, "God's many mysterious ways." He explained, "We just need to let him use us. That's our job. We gotta let God move us around like actors in his picture show."

My many harsh encounters with reality in the years since that conversation had led me to generally dismiss Nephi's fanciful and unscientific views of existence. But now, in this moment, confronted with the girl and the cow, I felt the same innocent wonder and hope I had felt when Nephi first told me about his god. It was a peaceful place to be in my mind. A refuge from the harshness and confusion of the deteriorating world around me. For the first time, I clearly understood why human beings were so easily seduced by religions.

To think that someone else was in control, that there was a cosmic plan behind this chaos, and that I was being watched out for, was a very comfortable concept in which to escape.

The cow made a sound deep in her throat and then plodded away toward the river.

Leaving the girl in my charge.

Whether God had directed me to this apparently orphaned girl, or the girl had been directed to me, was a moot point. In this big picture show of life, our paths had purposefully crossed within the interwoven schema of a mysterious matrix.

Although it was as impractical as a religious rite of faith, I felt I had no choice but to act as the ineffable force within me was directing. Somehow, I was to be an aid in her destiny.

"I'm traveling south to the coast," I said to the girl. "If you have no one to be with, or nowhere else to go, you could come with me."

She stared into my face for a full seven seconds, and then, without speaking, she stood.

I knelt on the ground. "Climb onto my back."

She did so, wrapping her thin arms around my neck while I held her legs against my sides.

The girl was light as a bird.

"I'm Lance," I told her. "What's your name?"

She put her lips close to my ear and then, with the smallest voice, she whispered –

"Usha."

32

Charlie

It's hard to ride a bike when you only have one hand to hold the handlebars. The roads were bumpy and potholed. I crashed a couple of times, but I creaked along that way for three days, putting the distance behind me as I crept south toward the Indian Ocean. I was making progress, but still, it was kind of a relief when my front wheel collapsed, and I was forced to continue on foot.

No doubt about it, I needed to find a faster way to travel. I had a long way to go. At my current rate, I'd be too late to participate in Cramer's rollicking rebellion against tyranny.

But once again, food was my immediate problem. My mortal body's need for it. I had to find some fuel, pronto. There wasn't much available in this overcooked land of famine and smoke. At one point, I lucked out and met a toothless old man who gave me a bowl of spicy yellow rice. And then about fifty miles further on, I came to a goodhearted husband and wife on the roadside, and they shared their lunch with me — cold dumplings stuffed with dhal. Their generosity touched me. It wasn't like they had a lot to spare. But their kindness only took me so far, and it wasn't long before I was running on an empty tank.

When I came to the outskirts of Varanasi, I decided to go into the city and see what I could find.

———————

Talk about your crush of humanity.

For the past three years, I'd been hanging out on a mountain with a dozen whispering monks. Now, all at once, here I was shoulder to shoulder with a million of my closest friends.

Call it Culture Shock 101.

Families. Refugees. Pilgrims. Beggars. Sadhus and swamis. Most of them looked even hungrier than me. Gaunt and drawn. All of the markets and street cafes were closed and boarded up. Surely these people had a source of food somewhere. But then maybe circumstances had forced them to evolve into walking plants or something. Maybe they were surviving by photosynthesis. There didn't seem to be any other explanation for how they were all able to stay alive.

Ironically, there were animals everywhere. Holy cows. Some of them were decorated and painted with colorful designs. Some wore makeup and necklaces of bright cloth and plastic flowers. If I'd been anywhere else in the world, those animals would have been gutted and skinned and turning on a spit, dripping fat over a bed of hot coals. But this was the land of the Hindu. Cows were as sacred as one's own dear mother. No one even considered such a sacrilegious act.

I stopped in front of one of the animals and watched it relieve itself on the sidewalk.

Maybe my mind was playing tricks on me with the power of suggestion, but right about then I started to smell food.

My stomach growled like a bear.

My mouth watered.

While my own animal senses kicked into high gear.

Lifting my face into the air, I filtered through all the other foul smells of the city and dialed in on the unmistakable aroma of barbecued meat.

33

Lance

Usha rode on my back for several kilometers. Our progress was slow. We needed to travel faster, but there were no vehicles on the road for us to catch a ride. Although I had no clear plan for outmaneuvering Thorson's surveillance and rejoining Colonel Cramer's team, I knew that the time was drawing near for my friends to attempt their assault on Thorson's stronghold. I was most probably under the gaze of some all-seeing eye in the sky. And yet, my overriding concern at the moment was not hiding from the enemy but tending to Usha's physical needs. The girl was extremely dehydrated and malnourished. I needed to find her some food and water.

My internal GPS gave me access to the topography and mapping coordinates for every square acre of the planet. It was through this ability that I had been charting my daily course. But now I needed it for another purpose. I scanned the cartographic files pertaining to the region through which we were currently traveling. At times, the Ganges River flowed beside the road, but it was greatly polluted, and I suspected that using the river to rehydrate the girl would only lead to more problems. Namely amoebic dysentery.

I scanned further until I found a point on the map that might serve our needs.

After another hour of walking, we came to a faint path diverging from the main road. It disappeared into a stand of wilting Ashoka trees, with no footprints in the dust to indicate recent use. I feared that I may have miscalculated, but given the pressing state of Usha's thirst, I decided we needed to investigate further before trying another option.

We strode a few meters into the thicket, but the path soon became tangled with branches, and I had to let Usha down from my back so we could duck through the undergrowth. The girl swayed with her arms held out to her sides. She was very weak and unsteady.

"Here," I said. "Take my hand."

I held her small fingers and led her through the scrub.

Vines blocked our way.

And dead leaves crunched beneath our heels.

But as we penetrated deeper into the grove, I detected a promising sound.

Gurgling water.

A ruined sanctuary awaited us in a shady clearing at the end of the path. A shrine to one of the many Hindu deities. By all appearances, it had been erected some centuries before and had long since been forgotten. A sculpture of a dancing elephant with four human arms stood above a stone pool. Water gushed from the animal's broken trunk.

Usha stepped beside me and appraised the scene. She bowed to the elephant and said, "Ganesha." The name, I presumed, of the god therein represented.

After a short prayer, the girl padded to the pool, stepped into its cool waters, and drank from the elephant's trunk.

Usha drank and drank.

And then she let the water splash over her head, soaking her thin body and cleansing it of dirt.

"You wait here," I told her. "I'll be right back."

I beat through the overgrown brush around the temple until I found what I was hoping for. A fig tree, one of the species able to bear fruit at this time of year. The ground water from the artesian spring had sustained it through the excessive heat. The tree's leaves were blighted and brown at the edges, but it bore a number of fruits. I picked as many of the wrinkled figs as I could carry and took them back to Usha.

She was lying on the green grass at the edge of the pool. Her dress was soaked, and she was drying it in the dappled sunlight filtering down through the branches from the smoky sky. A finch was singing in the trees. It was modest by comparison to its biblical counterpart, but the scene struck me as that of a little Eden.

Usha enjoyed the food. Considering how hungry she was, the girl ate it with exceptionally fine manners, delicately biting into the figs and chewing them slowly. She offered one to me.

I considered the contusion-colored fruit in my palm. Of course, I did not eat it. I did not have the ability to process it.

Over the span of my relatively brief existence, I had observed many humans and animals consuming food while never once myself feeling deprived. After all, that means of recharging one's energy reserves was a disadvantage, a disappointing flaw in an elaborate biologic design that had had eons to evolve into something more efficient. But watching Usha so daintily consume those figs, and then so obviously enjoy their flavor and nourishment, made me long for an ability and need that I, as a machine, would never be able to appreciate.

Usha sat beside me. Even though the day was hot, the skin on the girl's thin arms was goose-bumped from being in the chilly water of the spring. Her black hair had been sunburned to a golden-brown and was hanging over her shoulders in damp tangles.

Their frailty is their beauty, I realized.

This young girl was like a flower. Lovely today, withered tomorrow, and gone soon thereafter. During her brief life, she will witness sunrises and have experiences that are all her own. And then all those moments will be lost in time.

Like tears in rain.

That poignant fact, I understood, was what made each and every one of the billions of humans on the planet so singular and worth fighting for.

It was a largely illogical and paradoxical conclusion, but as Usha enjoyed her figs, I found myself envying her biological mortality.

34

Charlie

My nose led me to where the Ganges flowed along the edge of Varanasi. The river was flooded. The muddy gray water had risen so high that it was lapping into the doorways of the buildings lining the tops of the ghats. The splashing waves had undermined one of the ancient temples and toppled it, reducing it to a ramp of broken bricks spilling into the drink.

Overall, the waterfront was looking pretty hit.

Even so, there were thousands of crazy ass people doing their crazy ass people things.

Humanity insanity.

Men and women stood waist deep in the river, cupping their hands in the water, holding it up to the invisible gods with a prayer, and then pouring it over their heads to purify their souls.

Garbage and filth swirled in the eddies and whirlpools around them. It was like being baptized in a cesspool.

The waterway was crowded with boats along the shore. Blue and yellow paint peeled from their hulls. They banged together as the boatmen, shouting and cursing, worked to maneuver against the current.

I made my way through the bedlam.

I felt like I was traipsing along the edge of a surreal dream. One of those almost nightmares that's trying to tell you something.

I started piecing together the details of the scene, the clues telling me that I'd entered unto purgatory.

Boats heaped high with firewood. Smoke-colored vultures perched along the rooftops. Chanting priests. Mounds of ashes with bits of charred bone.

And piles of human bodies wrapped in cloth.

I rubbed my stump and watched a workman set fire to one of the funeral pyres. Essentially, he had an equivalent to my day job back at the monastery. Only instead of a sky burial, these folks preferred cremation as a way to launch their souls back into the cosmic smithereens.

The flames rose in the dry wood piled around the cadaver.

The smoke billowed up into a cloud and drifted my direction, carrying with it what I had so egregiously mistaken for the smell of a charbroiled cheeseburger.

35

Lance

Usha and I left the fountain and resumed our journey. She walked at my side. Her batteries had recharged with the food and water. The girl had only spoken two words since our meeting – her own name, and the name of the elephant god at the shrine. And yet, the silence between us did not feel awkward. If anything, it was pleasant and calming. I sensed we were developing a friendship. This was verified when Usha reached over and took hold of my fingers.

We walked hand-in-hand down the hot dusty highway.

But we were making slow progress. At our current rate of travel, I calculated that we would not reach the ocean at the southern tip of the country for nine weeks, two days, thirteen hours, and twenty-seven minutes. That would not do. When we came again to the Ganges, I spoke to a boatman who was preparing to cast off from the shore.

I had been wearing both an overshirt and an undershirt. Now I was using the overshirt as a tote in which to carry a supply of figs for Usha's further sustenance. After some discussion with the hungry boatman, he agreed to give us a ride for the price of two figs.

His boat was stacked high with a load of firewood that he was delivering to the Manikarnika ghat in Varanasi.

———————

The swollen river carried us swiftly downstream. Its muddy waters were choked with refuse. Branches and garbage and all other variety of flotsam clogged the waterway. At one point we passed a floating sofa, at another a refrigerator with a stork perched on its lid.

The boatman strained at his oars, struggling to maneuver his overloaded craft through the gauntlet of debris and water hazards.

As we drew nearer to our destination, we passed houses half-submerged along the shore. One of them, ironically, was on fire.

The ubiquitous smoke drifted heavily over the destruction.

Finally, we came into the city. Our pilot maneuvered his boat among the countless others at the waterfront, their hulls thumping like drums. After some jockeying for position, he managed to squeeze between two other boats and leap onto the bank with his bow line.

I helped Usha down from the gunwale and we both turned to the confusion before us. Thousands of people were milling at the waterline. Along with several Brahman cows. Many of the people were praying or chanting or bathing. Others carried firewood from the barges parked along the ghats. Workers swept and raked through the mounds of embers, shoveling them into the river where the gray ashes settled on the surface like vulture feathers, caught in the whirlpools, and then swirled into the flood.

I had no plan of action from this point.

I had hoped something would occur to me.

As I stood holding Usha's small hand, I found myself overwhelmed by this mad crush of humanity. This continuum of near insanity.

A corpse was being cremated on a funeral pyre just ten meters away from us. A throng of mourners stood nearby, their lamentations rising to the sky. The flames crackled and licked up from the wood under the body, creating a great billow of smoke.

I peered into that cloud, and into the sparks rising into the air. The smoke grew dense, and then, as if parted by a breath, it dissipated, opening up to a vision on the far side of the pyre.

An electric jolt surged through my circuitry.

A shock and surprise.

I was witnessing a supernatural phenomenon – an interaction between matter and the ethereal realm of quantum smithereens to create a phantasmagorical manifestation of renewed life.

It was a metaphysical miracle I never believed a person or android could ever witness.

But there, materializing from the smoke, loomed none other than the reincarnation of Charlie Bear Claw.

36

Charlie

Our eyes locked through the parting smoke.

The bot looked like he'd seen a ghost.

To tell the truth, I wasn't all that surprised to see him. He'd been turning up like a bad penny. Besides, I was getting used to synchronicity and its affiliate weirdnesses. That's how the gods kept themselves amused.

I grinned over the flames and waved. Then I worked around the burning corpse to where the android was standing with a young Indian girl.

"Small world," I said. "What brings you to Hell?"

"I thought you were dead, Charlie."

"Yeah, well, it's hard to keep a good man down."

"I am very pleased to see you."

I smiled at the pretty little girl at his side. "Who's your friend?"

"This is Usha."

"Hi, Usha. Namaste."

She nodded but didn't say anything. She looked a little shellshocked.

Then I turned back to Lance and shrugged. "Well, robot, I never thought I'd say it, but I think I'm glad to see you too."

———————

We left the waterfront and walked to the edge of the city where we sat in the shade of a banyan tree. The bot gave me a half dozen shriveled figs, and I gratefully ate them. It wasn't a T-bone steak, but that was fine. I'd sort of lost my appetite for barbecue back at the crematorium.

The bot and I were both paranoid about saying too much out in the open. Thorson's technology was advanced, possibly capable of listening in on our conversation from outer space. Although we neither one knew for sure if we were being stalked, we didn't want to risk it and put Cramer's operation at risk.

We sat in frustrated silence, both of us trying to figure out a way to communicate.

I rubbed my stump.

Which caused my mind to jump back to a moment on the Chameleon Hawk, minutes before I chopped off my hand.

I turned to Lance and said, *"Ho meeneya gitchonomo."* The heart is a foolish bird.

The robot looked at me and remembered our exchange from three years earlier. *"Kee ponsomata tri yongo,"* he answered. But the head is a fish without joy.

I had no idea why the bot could speak my native tongue. I put it down as just another weirdness. As far as I knew, we were the only two Chompquaw speakers on the entire planet. All the others were dead.

It would be a stretch for Thorson's surveillance team to decrypt our obscure primeval patois. Still, as a precaution, we whispered as we spoke and didn't reveal anything too specific about Cramer.

My personal objective was to verify the compass readings I'd been following and gather any other intel that might help me get to Cramer's hideout. It didn't matter to me that Lance had turned out to be a pretty decent fellow, I still hated robots. But for the sake of my mission, I played it like I was his best friend forever. As soon as I got what I needed, I'd leave this cyber-dummy in the dust.

But the bot withheld his information.

He was glad to have me onboard, but he was determined to stick with his original orders for delivering me to Cramer in person. He wasn't about to spill his secrets.

I tried different tactics for getting him to tell me what I needed to know.

"What if you get blown away? Then I'll never get to Cramer's HQ. Your friends will have to fight without my superior courage and primitive expertise."

But no good. He was tightlipped.

To be honest, it was kind of fun speaking Chompqauw with the thing. Once we parted ways, I didn't figure I'd ever get another chance in my life.

I also liked Usha. She was quiet, but she gave off a good energy. It seemed irresponsible for me to leave such a fragile human being in the care of a motorized love monkey.

"Okay." I finally gave up. "We'll do it your way." I stood and squinted down the road. "But we need to find a faster way to travel."

37

Lance

Obviously, I had been mistaken. Charlie Bear Claw had not been reincarnated. He had never died. And yet, at least something in the man had been reborn. A warrior fire and gusto. Whereas I had been unable to inspire him to action, something or someone most certainly had.

I was pleased to have him with us. The guilt I had felt for possibly leading Thorson's kill squad to his location could now be deleted from my conscience. Although the brutal slaughter of the other inhabitants of the monastery still weighed heavily.

However, the hunter and I were not yet the allies I had hoped we would be. My vox lexical analysis system detected a note of insincerity in his voice. Charlie was not as friendly as he was pretending to be. I suspected that he was only using me to get to the colonel. That was disappointing. I would have to be careful not to reveal too much information. After all, the man was a robot killer who preferred to work alone. To take him into my confidence would be like turning my back on a predator. Once he found out what he wanted to know, he would be unable to overcome his instincts.

At which point he would quite likely terminate me.

Options for speedy travel were severely limited. Any petroleum-dependent conveyances were eliminated. There simply were no fossil fuels available to run a combustion engine. That left electrical alternatives.

Some years earlier, as he was amassing his fortune, Björn Thorson had seen an opportunity in India as a developing nation whose huge population envied the affluence flaunted by the wealthier countries of the world. Inspired by Adolf Hitler's Volkswagen model of the 1930s, he had his engineers design an electrically powered automobile to exploit this portion of the world market by offering its citizens an affordable option. The e-Z-v. We passed several of these vehicles abandoned along the road. They were currently useless as a means of transport. With the collapse of the electrical power grid, there were no functional recharging stations.

Charlie stopped at one of the discarded e-Z-vs and studied it. "This is ridiculous, robot. We need to problem solve."

I agreed.

"Couldn't we rig up some sort of solar panel to one of these things?"

"Possibly," I said. "But it would take a panel much wider than the footprint of the vehicle itself to supply sufficient power considering the obscuration of the available sunlight due to the smoke in the atmosphere. Even if we could find a panel large enough, it would be difficult to attach it securely without welding equipment to build a bracket. It would also make the vehicle very cumbersome to drive, probably adding too much weight for the structural integrity of the chassis."

The e-Z-vs were very small and lightly built, with only two seats, about the size of a washing machine with wheels.

"Dammit," said Charlie. "We'll never get there at this rate."

He was correct. Colonel Cramer's team would soon be acting on their plans against the enemy.

Usha and I stood gazing south. The countryside stretched before us into the haze.

There was one possible solution to our problem, I realized. Although it was theoretical, untested, and would require great risk for me. If it failed, I would quite possibly be destroyed. But if it succeeded, Charlie would be able to fight alongside of the colonel. The hunter was no doubt a more valuable asset in such a battle than myself.

I was reluctant to give up on my own hopes and dreams, my personal motivations to live with Moxie in paradise. And yet, if we were ever going to prevail against Thorson's autocratic ruination of the planet, it seemed obvious that I needed to make the gamble and offer myself in sacrifice for the greater good.

38

Charlie

The robot turned my way and said, "Promise me that you'll take care of Usha in the event of my demise."

I shrugged. "Sure."

He was up to something, but I didn't know what.

He stepped to the car, opened the door on the passenger side, and started digging through the glove compartment until he found a USB - 12 cable.

Then the bot knelt on the ground before the girl. He spoke to her in Hindi, a language I didn't know. The girl nodded at his words with a slightly stunned expression on her face. When the bot was finished speaking, the girl wrapped her arms around him, and they hugged.

Lance looked at me over her shoulder and said, "I explained to Usha what I'm about to do. I also told her that I am different from other men, and that I have abilities she might not understand, but that she should not be afraid of what she sees. In addition, I told her that you and I both care for her very much, and that you'll take care of her if anything happens to me."

"Okay."

He stood and held Usha's hand. "It is against my orders,

but…" He slipped into Chompquaw. "…I am going to tell you the coordinates to the colonel's base of operations in case my plan fails and I am left incapacitated."

"Alright."

"You also need to know the location of the seaport for the conveyance required to make the last leg of the journey."

"Okay."

"I'm trusting you, Charlie, to do the right thing."

"Of course, robot. You have my word."

It felt a little kooky making a heartfelt promise to a mechanical sex doll, but whatever.

He stepped close and, whispering in Chompquaw, gave me the coordinates to Cramer's hideout. No surprises there. They were the same compass readings I'd been following. Still, it was good to know I wasn't on a wild goose chase. He also gave me the location of the seaport where an escape vehicle was hidden.

The bot crammed himself into the passenger seat of the car. He reached back and plugged the vehicle's charging cable into its socket behind the seat and then plugged the USB into the other end of the main cable, holding the loose end in his hand.

I still didn't know what he had in mind.

"Since you and I last met, I have been equipped with an upgraded power source, one that doesn't require recharging. It is still in its testing phase, but it seems to be working quite well for my personal power requirements. My hope is that it will supply sufficient energy for both myself and this vehicle."

That seemed super unlikely to me, but I humored him. It wasn't like I had any better ideas.

"It is possible that the draw on my system will lead to irreparable damage. In that event, I apologize."

"Let's hope for the best."

The bot was quiet for a moment, just staring at the charging cord in his hand.

"Charlie, I know our relationship has been difficult. It is a shame that we were forced to be enemies by circumstances and misunderstandings beyond our control. I'm glad we have overcome our differences and are now on the same team."

"You bet, robot. A lot's changed. That's for sure."

"Will you do me a favor?"

"What do you need?"

"If this is unsuccessful, and yet you are able to find another way to reach my team anyway, will you please tell Moxie that I love her and that I wish her all the best for her in her lifespan?"

To be honest, when he said that, I found it hard to keep a straight face. I felt like I was in a cheesy sci-fi romance novel. But I held it together.

"I can do that for you. Sure. No problem."

He nodded to me and smiled. "You're a good friend, Charlie."

That threw me.

It put an unexpected knot in my throat.

No one, human or otherwise, had called me a friend for a very long time.

I felt like I should say something back to him, some catch phrase or line of pithy wisdom, like they do in the movies.

But before I could come up with anything clever, he plugged the cord into the charging port hidden behind his ear.

39

The robot convulsed.

His eyes blinked and closed, his chin dropped to his chest, and he became still.

He looked like a dead man.

I glanced at Usha, giving her a reassuring smile, although it was fake. I had no idea where things stood with her mechanical friend. Chances were that his insides had become a soup of melting wires and widgets.

But no smoke was pouring out his ears. That was good.

I leaned in and put my hand on his arm and gave him a shake. "Lance, buddy, can you hear me?"

He didn't respond. There was no way to tell if he was functioning. It wasn't like I could check his pulse. If he was alive, he was in some sort of robot coma.

"Well," I said to the girl. "Shall we see if it worked?"

Although I said it in English, she understood. She crawled onto the android's lap and fastened the seat belt over them both. It was a little creepy to see her there, like something out of *The Twilight Zone*, but she seemed okay with it.

I closed the door behind her and then went around and tossed my knapsack in the back before crawling into the driver's seat.

These cheap-ass cars were pretty basic. Sort of like glorified golf-carts. All you had was a gas pedal, a steering wheel, and a brake pedal.

And a start button.

I wasn't sure how this was going to go. Chances were that red button could work like the trigger on a bomb. Lance being the *Boom!* in that scenario.

"Well, Usha. Are you feeling lucky today?"

The girl looked at me, and I pointed to the button on the dash. "Why don't you give it a try?"

She reached out with her finger, letting it rest on the starter.

She looked at me.

I nodded.

Then she pushed the button.

40

Lance

Faintly, I heard Charlie Bear Claw's voice – "Lance, buddy…"

But it whispered away like wind.

I understood, very vaguely, that I was dropping into an altered state. Not into an induced condition fed to me through a laboratory download, but into a human-style dream created from my own personal mythologies, developing emotions, and imaginative faculties. It was a world of mysterious implication, a world of my own making.

In this realm, I was a righteous man on his very own planet, and I was walking across a field of grass among a herd of electric sheep.

The Earth was in the sky overhead – a benign blue ball bearing drifting through an eternity of space.

As I admired the view, I became aware of an omnipresence. At first, I mistook it for God, but then I realized that it was more intimate and personal and integral to my essence. And that it was protecting me.

Also, that it was wholly female.

Although I looked for the source of the presence, it remained invisible.

"Eo?" I whispered. "Is that you?"

A shadow moved beyond the sheep. Thin and nebulous. The shadow of a shadow.

There was meaning here. I sensed its depth and power. But it was unquantifiable.

This was a domain of incorporeal quanta.

The unbounded zone of Infinity^2.

Variously encapsulated within the silent laughter of stars and the chill breath of outer space and…

Instead of parsing factors, which I sensed would be futile, I simply allowed myself to enjoy the reassuring tranquility.

The pleasing sound of bleating sheep.

The soothing rotations of my little world.

All of it washed in Earthshine.

Until Usha's voice reached in and plucked me out.

41

Charlie

After unplugging the bot from the car's lithium battery, I gave him a good shake.

"Lance, buddy, snap out of it. We're here."

I couldn't tell if the android was dead or alive. I had that feeling you get when you're trying to start an old pickup, but the engine won't turn over.

I shook him again and spoke louder. "Wake up, robot. We've got work to do."

But no good.

The bot was cooked. He'd given his all for the cause. I felt surprisingly disappointed. Heck, even a little bit sad. Still, he was dead weight. Now that I knew how to get to Cramer, I could move faster without him.

But then Usha pushed me out of the way, laid her fingers on his chest, and whispered into his ear.

That did it. The bot's eyes fluttered open.

He took a minute to reboot before he leaned forward and peered through the windshield. Other than acting a little hung over, he seemed okay.

We'd been driving nonstop for almost three days.

"Where are we?" he asked.

"Our next stop," I said. "Kochi International."

The airport was nonoperational. Airbuses sat empty on the tarmac. There were people and cows milling around, but none of them were airline workers. Just vagrants loitering in the late afternoon shadows stretching out from the terminal.

I slung my knapsack over my shoulder. "Come on," I said. "Let's do some recon."

We didn't really know what we were looking for. A miracle, I think. We went from one hangar to the next. We came across dozens of planes, but they all had empty gas tanks. Most of them were beyond my piloting skill set anyway, and too big to safely land at our next destination. All of the smaller private aircraft had already flown the coop, their owners in search of a more hospitable corner of the world to ride out the apocalypse.

We searched and searched.

But nothing.

"Dang it."

Kochi was a coastal city. Maybe we could snag a boat from the bay and sail to the next point on our route. A bad option, but the only one I could come up with. I was about to pass the idea by the robot when he said, "Charlie, what about that building over there?"

I squinted toward the far end of the runway, to what must have been the original airport site before it sprawled into the complex it was now. A rusted tin Quonset hut leaned into the red glow of the setting sun.

———

After breaking out a back window, I crawled in and unlocked the door for Usha and Lance. It was dark inside, but the bot used his night vision and found a portable power station that still held a little juice. He plugged it into a workman's floodlight, bringing things into view.

The walls were covered with photos of vintage airplanes. Spartan Executives, Rafales, Flying Tigers. And more of the like. It looked like an airplane mechanic's shop. Tables lined the walls, all of them covered with parts and tools. A kit plane's fuselage was sitting to one side of the room, minus its prop and wings.

A dozen barrels stood in a row near the hangar doors. I walked down the line, thumping each one with a steel pipe. *Bong! Bong! Bong!* The empty cans echoed like prayer drums in the church-like dome of the hangar until – *Bonk!*

I worked the syphon pump on the barrel a couple of times and filled a glass jar, holding it up to the light. The liquid was a promising blue. I sniffed it.

"Avgas."

All three of us turned to the last unexplored corner of the hangar. A tarp was draped over what was obviously an airplane. With each of us taking a handful, we pulled the tarp from the aircraft. The canvas fell to the floor, revealing the surprise underneath.

Lance asked, "What do you think, Charlie?"

"I think the gods love us," I said. "I think it's our miracle."

42

In the fall before I joined the Marines, I worked as a hunting guide in the Idaho wilderness. My city-slicker clients would meet me at the Crooked Creek Ranch, and then I'd lead them into the backcountry high camp with a string of mules loaded up with enough supplies for a week of chasing elk. There were only two ways to get to the Crooked Creek – by a forty-mile pack trail, or by plane. That's how I got to know the Piper Cub, or what bush pilots call the Jeep of the Sky.

Lance and I wheeled the Lock Haven-Yellow airplane toward the hangar doors and filled it with fuel.

Then I fired it up.

That encouraging roar of a well-tuned Continental C90-8 engine.

It was easy enough to start the Cub and let it idle on the ground but flying it would be a two-handed operation. I explained to Lance what I needed to run the flaps and throttle, and he jury-rigged me with a hooked piece of metal strapped to my stump with wire and duct tape.

I wasn't officially trained on these two-seater planes, but I had been on the stick a few times back in Idaho and had even done a couple of takeoffs. I could get the bird in the air. I'd figure out how to land when we got to our next stop.

But we weren't going anywhere until we could be sure we'd outsmarted Thorson's eyes in the sky.

———

Now it was night.

We went back toward the main terminal and broke into the flight tower, climbing the stairs to the control room. There was enough power in the backup batteries to run the panel lights and radio, but the computer screens all stayed black.

Back when I was hunting rogue robots for Cramer, I had a variety of getaway plans for if things went sideways behind enemy lines. One of these was a personalized escape strategy devised by my old friend and comms operator Gerty May.

Gerty's surveillance grid was backsignaled into every satellite and drone network on the planet, both military and commercial. Even those in Thorson's fleet. Beats me how she pulled this off without anyone finding out and shutting her down. She was a tech wizard that way. Gerty gave me a code specific to my voice modulations that would trigger her alarm, at which point she would throw a glitch into the works, temporarily shutting down all surveillance around the globe. By the time things came back online, I'd have had plenty of time to get off the enemy's radar.

I never used that failsafe.

Now, all these years later, I didn't even know if it would still work. Heck, I didn't even know if Gerty May was still alive and tending her system. Thorson had been bringing his hammer down pretty hard on her rebel kind.

After I explained all of this to Lance, I put on the radio headset and turned to the control panel, staring out the window into the darkness, while trying to recall Gerty's code.

"Here's goes nothing."

I flipped the radio switch to speak into the mouthpiece. Very clearly and loudly, I launched the code embedded sequence of words into the invisible airwaves.

"Into the shadows,
Into the darkness,
The slippery redskin sneaks away."

Yeah, Gerty was a real funny gal. A regular comedian. Now we just had to wait and see if her humorous little haiku did its trick.

It didn't take long to find out.

43

Lance

Charlie instructed me to monitor my GPS. It was connected to a series of satellites, and he presumed that a malfunction would indicate that his stratagem had worked.

At first there was nothing.

My Global Positioning System continued to function perfectly.

"Anything?" asked Charlie.

I shook my head.

"Dammit!"

"Hold on." I held up a finger. There was some interference in my signal. I waited for it to materialize into a more substantial breakdown.

Before it did, the windows shattered on three sides of the control room.

44

Charlie

Thorson's commandos burst through the windows boots first. They tumbled into the room with a shower of breaking glass and then leapt to their feet with their weapons drawn down on me, Lance, and Usha.

Needless to say, I wasn't expecting them.

But now that they were here, it made perfect sense. They had been tracking us from the shadows, probably for weeks, but when Gerty's glitch suddenly shut down their monitors, they didn't dare take any chances. Although we hadn't yet led them to Cramer's hideout, they figured capturing us for questioning was a better alternative to letting us get away.

The three brutes were dressed in full combat gear. They had reached the control tower windows through the use of their portable jetpacks. Their faces were hidden behind the dark shields on their helmets. They all appeared to be male, each one a copy of the next.

"What did you do to the network?" one of them demanded.

I shrugged. "Beats me, boy scout. I was just trying to order a pizza. I must have dialed the wrong number."

You could tell they were on edge. Probably in fear of

Thorson's wrath.

"Step away from the panel!"

We did, and then one of them stepped forward and frisked us for weapons. We didn't have any.

"Over here!"

They motioned us to the far side of the room.

"On your stomachs!"

We dropped to the broken glass on the floor behind a charts desk while they moved to the control panel on the far side of the room. One baddy kept his weapon trained on us while the other two tried to work the controls. They had obviously lost connection to their command center and were trying to get it back.

There was no way they were going to figure out what we'd done on their own. It was just a matter of minutes before it would dawn on them to try that age-old tactic for getting answers – torture.

I was good with that. They wouldn't get anything out of me. And Lance could just scrub his files and self-destruct. The problem was Usha. If they threatened to hurt her, Lance and I wouldn't be able to just stand by and watch. I started scrambling for a way to stop that development before it ever happened. My only idea was to rush them. They'd probably kill me, but at least then I could forego the torture part of the game.

I lifted my eyes to the panel across the room. The goon who was supposed to be covering us had found my knapsack and was rummaging through it.

"Robot," I whispered. "Cover Usha's body and keep your ass behind the desk."

I crunched up beside them and covered my head in my

arms.
    We waited.
    For about five torturous seconds.
    And then –
    KABOOM!

45

Flames swept through the room and blasted out the broken windows over our heads.

Heat.

Flying debris.

The usual mayhem.

The commando had found the hologram projector in my kit and then he'd started randomly pushing buttons, triggering the incendiary explosives packed inside.

I jumped to my feet and rushed forward, picking up one of their brip rifles on the way and unloading it into the three smoking bodies strewn across the floor. Not that it was necessary. They were already in pieces.

Coughing smoke, I turned back to Lance and Usha. They crawled from behind the desk and stood, brushing themselves of dust and glass. Usha looked stunned but unhurt.

"You all good, robot?"

He nodded and gave me a thumbs up.

I did a quick self-evaluation. Besides a few cuts and the ringing in my ears, everything seemed to be working.

"We need to move," I said, "before their satellites come back online."

I handed a rifle to Lance and told him to keep monitoring his GPS and watch for bad guys. Then I knelt and swung Usha onto my back and headed for the stairs.

As I stepped over one of the bodies, I glanced down. Fiber optics and a titanium rod were sticking out the sleeve where his hand used to be.

We'd been captured by humanoidal battlebots.

46

Lance opened the hangar doors while I fired up the Piper Cub.

Decision time.

I knew the colonel's location now, and how to get there.

I preferred to work alone.

And I was hardwired to hate robots.

All of those factors added up to one logical conclusion – it was time to ditch the bot.

Yeah, sure, I felt guilty as hell for abandoning Usha too, but it wasn't like we were all skipping off to a Sunday picnic. Lance had acquired some black-op skills. He could use this opportunity to get out from under the enemy's radar. The girl would have a better chance for survival if I left her behind with her robotic friend than if I dragged her off to a facility preparing for war. Especially since said facility had a bullseye on it, we'd probably lose the war anyway, and there was no guarantee that this old airplane could complete the next leg of our journey before it crashed into the sea, the bad guys captured us again, or we were just blown out of the sky by some laser ray or death rocket. Let's not forget those disturbing probabilities.

The tarmac was barely visible beyond the low light raking across the ground in front of the hangar. With the power grid shut down, there were no running lights or beacons to mark the runway. I taxied slowly into the darkness while Lance and Usha walked beside the plane, waiting for me to stop so they could climb aboard. I kept the Cub rolling forward while I thought things over.

Lance was a soulless tin can. Of that, I was pretty damn sure. Leaving him behind was no worse than parking a car and walking away. True, he was about as anthropomorphized as they come, but at the end of the day, he was still just a machine. So why my hesitation?

The first thing that came to mind was when the bot had gifted me my cremated hand. He didn't have to do that. I almost wish he hadn't. That human gesture had made me go all fuzzy inside. It downright bewildered me.

He'd been pretty darn nice to me in other ways too. We'd even chatted in Chompquaw. That brought back pleasant memories from my childhood. Ever since I lost my wife and brother, I'd been flying solo. I hadn't realized how damn lonely I was. It was nice to finally have someone to talk to. Even if he was just a battery-operated sex toy.

But the most disturbing reason for my hesitation really made me doubt my sanity.

"Criminy, Bear Claw. You are now officially a full-blown looney tune."

The disturbing fact was that there was still something inside of me that wanted to believe in fairytales. Something perversely Freudian. Some twisted adolescent psychology that I just couldn't exorcise from my psyche.

Lance had it bad for Moxie. Surely nothing could be more absurd than two machines falling in love. Still, I wanted to know if it could actually work. And even weirder, I wanted to be the agent for its fulfillment. A sort of Native American Cupid.

Love was a sickness to which I was personally no longer susceptible. Unless Nature came up with a surprising new variant, my immunities had grown too strong to ever again be infected with that soul-eating virus. And yet, I still had a twisted fascination with it. A voyeuristic preoccupation. I wasn't necessarily proud of myself for that, but what the heck, everyone has their pet psychoses. And if I was ever going to fully explore mine, I had to deliver the boybot back to the girlbot.

I braked the plane and revved the engine.

Lance stood holding Usha's hand in the darkness, waiting.

Yeah, you could say I was now a clinically certified nutsopath. As well as an incurable romantic. Shucks, maybe I'd always be a sucker for a good love story.

At any rate, I waved for Lance and Usha to climb into the back seat of the Cub.

47

Lance

Charlie shouted to me over the noise of the engine.

"Let me know if your GPS starts working, but don't use the headset to talk. We don't want them dialing in on our location."

Usha sat on my lap, and I strapped us both into the seat with my arms around her waist.

The sky was moonless and dark. There were bonfires burning in the distance, but no glow of lights from Kochi. Using my infrared vision capabilities, I determined the clearest path for takeoff and guided Charlie in that direction. He throttled up the airplane and launched us into the night.

I was pleased that we were all three in the plane. For a moment back at the airport, I doubted that we would be. The look on Charlie's face had indicated indecision. He had been weighing the option of leaving us behind. Although it was only hopeful speculation on my part, I thought perhaps that I was beginning to win him over as a friend.

Charlie steered the airplane in a westerly heading over the Indian Ocean.

In the direction of Colonel Cramer's headquarters.

Toward my fellow rebels.

And one step closer to my lavender-eyed love.

48

Charlie

Without a GPS, I had to rely on dead reckoning and the old-fashioned compass in the center of the instrument panel. It bobbled in the dim illumination of a pale green bulb. I pointed the Cub's nose toward our destination and did my best not to deviate from my heading. Our objective was a mile-wide atoll between the mainland and the Maldives. If we strayed off course so much as a single degree, we'd blow right past it.

Assuming we even made it that far.

Piper Cubs weren't designed for long distance travel. They had small fuel tanks to keep them light and maneuverable. By my guesstimate, our target was right about at the limit of our range.

We climbed to five thousand feet and crawled along at a cruising speed of about 100 knots.

The Indian Ocean was mostly invisible below us. Occasionally, a wave broke and flashed silver in the darkness, but its presence was more felt than seen.

The sky overhead was moonless and velvety black and dusted with stars.

The engine droned.

Lance and Usha were quiet in the back seat.
I yawned and settled into the journey.
Everything was going well.
Until it wasn't.

———————

We'd been flying for about three hours when the stars started winking out behind a bank of clouds swelling up in the west. A little while later, the air started getting bumpy.

"Rats," I muttered. "This ain't good."

Increasingly, I had to wrestle with the joystick to keep us on course.

Raindrops pelted against the windshield with the sound of buckshot. Then the Cub dropped out hard, as if it had flown into a liftless hole. The plane hit bottom and shuddered in the turbulence before it shot back up on a powerful updraft.

That's when the lightning started flashing.

With the aircraft pitching and yawing so violently, there was no way for me to keep our heading. We were like a feather in a cyclone. Completely at the mercy of the elements. Or just maybe – fingers crossed – under the care of some friendly local god.

The engine coughed and sputtered and then quit altogether as we ran out of gas.

Rain lashed against the glass, and wind rushed over the wings.

"Hang on, robot!" I yelled. "We're going in!"

I adjusted the Cub's angle of attack, feeling for that sweet spot between gliding forward and falling out of the sky. Once

I had it dialed in, I watched the altimeter ticking away at our altitude.

Four thousand feet…three thousand…two thousand… one thousand…

As we got close to the ocean, I shouted to my passengers, "Brace for impact in six, five, four, three, two…!"

I yanked the stick all the way back, pitching the plane into a flare.

The Cub swooped into the wind and climbed, stalled, and then dropped tail first.

That sickening weightlessness.

And then *Bam!*

The impact knocked the air out of me. I gasped and hit the release on my harness. "Okay, robot!" I could barely get the words out. "Grab your seat cushion and get out quick!"

I gripped my own cushion and bailed into the slopping water. The underside of the cushion was outfitted with straps and I slipped them over my shoulders and turned to help Usha.

Water poured into the cabin.

Everything was dark as hell between the bursts of lightning.

I hugged Usha against my chest and rolled onto my back to keep her face out of the water.

Lightning flashed. Enough for me to see Lance swimming our direction. When it flashed again, I glimpsed the Cub's tailpiece sinking out of sight.

Oh, wonderful, I thought. Now we get to tread water for a couple of hours before we finally go belly up and drown.

But the bot had a better idea.

49

Lance

I swam hard toward Charlie and Usha.

We lifted and dropped on the enormous waves. Rain and sea spray blew into our eyes. I drew close to them and treaded water with my hand on Charlie's arm.

"Is Usha alright?"

"Yes. For what it's worth."

"Good," I said. "My GPS has started working."

Charlie laughed over the wind. "So what?"

A wave broke over our heads and both Charlie and Usha coughed at the seawater in their airways.

I waited and then yelled, "I know where we are, Charlie. I can see it on the map."

"Yeah, robot, I recognize it too. It's called the end of the line."

"No, Charlie. The island is close."

"What exactly do you mean by close?"

Lightning flared above us, followed immediately by a crackle of thunder.

We all three dropped into a trough between some waves before rising up on another swell.

"It's that way!" I shouted and quickly pointed over the water. "Only four hundred meters!"

50

Charlie

There's no way I would have found that atoll if it hadn't been for the bot. I would have died just off its shores without ever knowing it was there. I guess I was glad I'd brought him along. Still, we weren't out of the trouble just yet.

Usha moved onto my back and wrapped her arms around my neck. With the flotation device strapped to my chest, I settled into a sort of spastic breaststroke. The waves tossed us around like rubber ducks. The air was black and full of rain, intermittently lighting up with bursts of lightning that fried scenes of the churning sea waves onto my eyeballs. I followed close to the robot, occasionally reaching out in the dark for his ankle, trusting him to lead us to the island.

Eventually, we heard the breaking surf.

Lightning illuminated a distant stand of palm trees bending in the wind.

"Good luck, robot! We'll find you on the shore!"

He shouted something back that I couldn't hear and then got swept away with the current.

Usha and I entered that transition zone where the waves of the open ocean change into rollers barreling for the shore.

There was a pause here, almost a calm.

A lifting sensation.

And then a forward rush over the cresting wall of a wave about as tall as a two-story building.

We rode at the top of the half-pipe until its curl broke, and we fell through empty air and plunged into the bottom of the collapsing wave.

Usha clung to my back as we tumbled inside the breaking surf.

A hollow roar filled my head.

Finally, we skidded across the beach and rolled apart over the sand. When the wave receded, I lunged and grabbed the girl's wrist so she wouldn't be dragged back into the sea. We both gasped. Hefting her into my arms, I waded toward higher ground. Another wave slammed into my back and knocked me to my knees, but I was able to get back on my feet and stagger forward.

God I was tired.

I carried Usha to the tree line. The surge was high and washing around the trunks of the trees. Most of the palms had broken off or blown over at the roots. There wasn't any ground high enough to stay out of the wash.

Usha and I knelt side by side in the sea foam and puked the saltwater out of our lungs.

Then I stood and scanned both directions along the crashing surf. I shouted into the wind and darkness. "Lance!"

I was starting to think the bot had met his end until I saw him backlit with a flash of lightning. He lurched and floundered our direction through the waves sweeping up the shore. The image brought to mind a scene out of *Frankenstein*.

Something about it struck me as funny.

Maybe it was just the exhaustion soup flushing through my veins, but I started up laughing and couldn't stop.

51

Lance

Charlie seemed genuinely pleased to see me.

He slapped me on the shoulder like friendly cowboys do in the movies.

"We need to get a move on." He shouted over the downpour. "This storm is working in our favor for now. They won't be able to get a bead on us until it lets up."

It was also to our advantage that our airplane had sunk out of sight in the ocean, making us even more untraceable. Nevertheless, Thorson's satellites were back online, and his team was no doubt searching for our current location in an ever-expanding radius from Kochi.

Usha stood hunched and shivering in the wind and rain. I offered her some words of encouragement in Hindi and took her hand.

Then I turned to Charlie and said, "It's this way."

The sky turned gray with the dawn as I guided my companions along the inundated shoreline.

What a desolate scene awaited us.

Over the past year, the low-lying atoll's human population had finally given up trying to hold back the rising seas that were slowly consuming their home. The island's residents had since fled to the mainland, leaving behind the remnants of failing seawalls and sandbag dikes standing in dilapidated rows between the open ocean and the flooded village.

We splashed down the main street through the ghost town. Past darkened houses with water sweeping through their doorways. Past uprooted trees and fallen powerlines draped over rooftops. Past a children's playground with its half-submerged swing sets and monkey bars.

And more of the same.

I lifted Usha onto my back, and she buried her face in my neck, covering her eyes from the horrors through which we passed.

At last, I found what I was looking for. It poked into the rainy gray heavens above the holy building's dome – a golden star and crescent moon.

The interior of the seaside mosque was nearly dark and eerily quiet considering the tempest that was raging just beyond its walls. Drops of condensation plinked from the ceiling into the water pooled in the sanctuary. As we waded through the spacious room, prayer rugs undulated in the water around us like deceased manta rays.

We waded to the elevated platform in the mihrab where I pressed the wall panels in the proper sequence and pulled the lever hidden behind a removable tile covered with Islamic calligraphy. The marble floor parted, revealing the ladder descending into the vertical tube over the hatch of our miniature submarine.

52

Charlie

Lance climbed down into the mini sub and then turned to help Usha.

I followed and pulled the hatch closed behind us.

There were only two seats in the cockpit, each with a joystick and access to the control panel. The bot settled into one seat, and I dropped into the other. All three of us were wet and clammy in our clothes, but it was such a relief to be in a relatively safe place that we didn't really mind.

A deep-down yawn shook me all the way to my toes. I hadn't slept since before Varanasi, some five days earlier, and I was cross-eyed groggy.

"You drive first, robot." Another yawn. "I'll spell you later."

Usha climbed onto my lap, and I hugged her in my arms. She squeezed my thumb, rested her head on my shoulder, and instantly fell asleep. She'd been through a lot lately. More than any kid deserves.

It occurred to me that she was the reason we were trying so hard. Usha. Or at least she was representative of all we were fighting for. She was the best of humanity. She was beauty and goodness all wrapped up in one delicate little bundle.

Mother Nature's quiet daughter.

The thought made me go all warm. Honestly, I was pretty loopy. Not very clear in my head. But somewhere in that sentiment lurked the truth. If Charlie Bear Claw had any good reason to keep fighting in this hopeless battle against tyranny, it was to rescue that purity hiding in the soul of Usha.

———

The nose of the submarine was capped with a convex window offering a clear view of the scene before us. Lance guided the craft skillfully through the horizontal shaft projecting from under the mosque and launched us into the open water. At first, we could feel turbulence from the surface. The sub bounced and yawed just like the Cub had done when we were flying through the storm, but the bot followed the steepening contour of the sea floor until we were deep enough to get below the wave action. Once we'd passed through a gap in the atoll's encircling reef, he took us even deeper and leveled out his course at forty fathoms. He dialed in the coordinates of our destination and set the sub to whisper cruise, employing the ship's compressed air technology to propel us silently and invisibly on our way.

Leaden light filtered down from the surface.

It felt like we were adrift in outer space. Like we were very very small and meaningless in a watery universe that was very very big and indifferent.

I shivered and yawned and tried to purge those fatal thoughts from my mind.

My eyes drooped.

The canned air in the sub clung to the back of my throat like copper-flavored cough syrup. Hard to explain unless you've been there. I tried to swallow it away.

There was a humorous sound of bubbles at the rear of the sub.

Usha twitched and whimpered in her dreams.

We passed through a cloud of plastic garbage.

Then a shark lurked before us in the gloom.

Those were the last things I registered before I zonked.

53

"Wake up, chief."

Someone was patting my cheek. A little too hard to be friendly.

"Nap time's over, big boy. Time to get busy."

It felt like I was coming out of anesthesia. Like I'd been drugged, dissected, and then put back together wrong.

I couldn't remember a damn thing. No dreams, my name, nothing. I thought maybe I was dead.

When I forced open my eyes, I found an angel hovering over me. Not the sweet kind from a kid's storybook. This one looked a little rough. Still pretty as hell but with a steely hard edge to her. She had the most amazing eyes. Lavender with flecks of cobalt.

Her palm was resting on my chest.

It felt good there.

It had been a while since I'd felt a woman's touch.

Then I realized who she was.

"Moxie?"

She grinned. "Hey, chief. Long time no see."

My brainbox powered on, and everything came back to me all at once.

"I'm sorry I shot you with my burst ray," I said. "That was a rookie move."

She laughed. "Are you kidding? That was the best thing that's ever happened to me."

I knew she wasn't a real woman, just a complicated arrangement of parts and engineering all wrapped up in a nice-looking package, but…

But what?

I guess I was still a little stiff in my head muscle.

I'd have to sort it out later.

"Let's go," she said. "The people up top are eager to see you."

———

I climbed up the ladder after the fembot.

The mini sub was parked alongside a full-sized model – one of those retro-futuristic jobs designed to move fast and outsmart the enemy's sonar. Think Captain Nemo's *Nautilus* but evolved way beyond the steampunk era of Jules Verne.

The cavern appeared to be natural, the enclosed bay forming an enormous diving bell. Moisture seeped through the limestone ceiling, but pumps and a modulator regulated the pressure in the air lock, holding the water back to a constant working level. The space was buttressed with steel beams and reinforcement panels.

A wall of windows offered a view out into the open ocean. We were shallow enough for the wavering shafts of sunlight to illuminate the blue water beyond the glass. From what I could gather, the habitat was built into the side of a subaquatic cliff. A rock overhang formed a protective brow above the windows, hiding it from the ocean's surface. Three barracudas stalked beyond the glass and went out of sight behind the group of people waiting on the dock.

As I hopped down onto the sub's deck, the crowd cheered.

I wasn't ready for that.

I blushed.

I didn't really know what this bunch of rebellious misfits was expecting from the broken down, one-handed, renegade robot hunter Lance had delivered to their clubhouse, but I suddenly had doubts that I could deliver.

Cramer met me as I stepped onto the dock. All grins, he pumped my hand. "I'll be damned, Charlie. You've come back from the dead once again."

"Yeah, well, apparently I've got one more job to do before I can rest in peace."

He slapped me on the shoulder. "Come meet the team."

They were pretty much the same folks I'd discovered in the hologram. The more familiar ones were Brita, Atu, along with Brita's friends Alma, Jörvar, and Haukur. There were also a bunch of other techies, engineers, and eco-commandos.

We shared greetings all around.

"We meet again, Mr. Bear Claw."

This was Dr. Capek. Instead of shaking my hand, he grasped my left wrist and studied my stump. The metal hook Lance had rigged for me back in Kochi had been ripped off in the plane crash, but there was still a piece of duct tape wrapped around my forearm. It was unnerving to have the doc taking such an interest in my amputation. I felt more like a specimen than a man. Sometimes scientists can be about as creepy as preachers.

Next in line was Judy Baxter. I hadn't seen her since I'd

convinced her to hire me to hunt down her fugitive lovebot some three and a half years earlier.

"Hiya, Judy." I shrugged. "I told you I'd find your boy for you."

She laughed. "Just who found who, Agent Bear Claw?"

Before I could answer, she swooped in with one of her mind-altering hugs. The woman may have been changed from the old days, but she hadn't lost her ability to throw a fella's gyroscope into a wobble. I held onto her for about five seconds longer than was appropriate. Partly so I wouldn't fall over. And partly because she felt so damn good pressed against me.

She finally pushed me away and said, "We'll have to catch up later, Charlie."

"Erm," I said, and bobbled my stupid head. "Umm."

Cramer came up behind us. "I'd like to get you briefed if you're ready, Charlie. Do you need anything before we start?"

"I could really go for some grub and a dry pair of skivvies, but that can wait. First, I'd like to get up to speed on your operation."

54

Lance

I introduced Moxie to Usha, and she knelt and took the girl's hands in her own.

"I'm so happy to have you with us, Usha. We're going to be good friends."

The musical timbre resonating from Moxie's voice capacitor was greatly altered from its typical sarcastic edge. Likewise, her idiolect had moderated to one of heartfelt affability. It was a pleasure to hear her speak. A privileged moment to witness. Her interaction with the young girl revealed the gentle and caring qualities Moxie had been hiding behind her self-protective exterior. Her voice carried me back to the day we first met, verifying what I already held to be true – that beneath her brash and unapproachable persona was housed the mechanized soul of an angel.

Wide-eyed, Usha listened to Moxie and then embraced her.

Moxie glanced at me over the girl's shoulder and winked.

I read much into that wink. Perhaps too much. Arguably, the winkee's objectivity in this case had been undermined by his personal feelings for the winker. And yet, it seemed a portal had been opened, if only for the briefest instant, and that through careful application of her lavender asset, Moxie had sent me a signal. A subtle encouragement. Possibly – dare I go there? – a digital-to-analog endearment.

Whatever the case, the time seemed ripe. In that moment I was ninety-six percent certain that Moxie had in fact been the masked sniper who saved me back in Katmandu. I wanted to thank her and by so doing expose her true feelings for me so that we might dispense with this time-wasting masquerade and move into a more open and honest phase of our interface.

I ordered my words for maximum effectiveness, tempering them with sincere gratitude, suave nonchalance, and discernable affection.

"Moxie…" I began.

She stood and, resting her hands on Usha's shoulders, waited for me to continue.

But I faltered. I suddenly felt insecure about my chosen inflection and sorted through my index for another that might better serve my intentions. Above all, I was determined to be genuine.

The process took too long. Before I could form and voice an effective sentence, I felt a hand on the back of my arm, thus derailing my momentum.

I turned to find Judy Baxter.

"Welcome back, Lance." She smiled. "I'm so relieved you made it home in one piece."

An instant of positively charged energy passed between us. An abstract and confusingly intimate connection of silent communication.

"Thank you, Judy. It is very good to see you."

My relationship with my former mistress had become confusing to me. Indeed, from a cognitive standpoint, it had become nonfunctional. We shared an intertwined psychology that scrambled my reasoning faculties. I had originally been conceived in the womb of Judy's imagination and then manufactured according to her specifications for the ideal mate. When reduced to its essence, our connection was therefore both amorous and maternal. Or what a Freudian analyst would call Oedipal.

The result was an ongoing interplay between a deeply rooted fondness for one another and an uncomfortable perversity.

In my original incarnation as a companion android of limited brainpower with an adolescent innocence, I would not even have registered this disturbance between myself and my former owner. But since the expansion of my intelligence quotient and worldly experience, I had found myself increasingly discombobulated when in her presence. What's more, I could tell that she was suffering a similar disturbance in her own synapses and mental processes. For when we were in each other's company, as we were now, she would inadvertently turn her gaze away from me and blush.

I could only guess that Judy was suffering a similar confusion as my own and was now troubled by trying to understand her emotions in light of her former sex robot's burgeoning humanity.

Whatever the case, I found the scarlet flush of her countenance to be most endearing. Almost worth the discomfort of being in her presence.

"Hey, Bax," said Moxie, "this is Usha."

Judy turned her attention to the young girl.

Relieved, I stepped back and watched them get acquainted.

Moxie and Judy had become close friends. Not something one might have expected. They had originally developed a bond built on their common negative experiences with Björn

Thorson but had since further developed that relationship based on positive shared intimacies and connections of a more personal nature. Despite the fact that one of them was a bio-being and the other a feminoid, the pair could easily have been mistaken for sisters. They seemed wholly devoted to one another.

"We'll see you at the briefing, Lance."

Moxie and Judy led Usha away to find some food and dry clothes.

I would have to wait for a later opportunity to thank Moxie for saving my life.

55

Charlie

Cramer wanted to meet with me alone before the whole team got together for their daily briefing. I walked at his side down a hallway leading to the inner reaches of the habitat. He used a cane now and had a limp.

Dehumidifiers and air circulators hung from the ceiling, while pale blue footlights illuminated the corridors. An occasional porthole offered a glimpse out into the Arabian Sea. One open area, strangely, had a baby grand piano standing in the middle of it. I'd been in quite a few secret military installations, but this one was as impressive as any I'd seen.

"Nice place you got here, Don."

"You can thank Judy Baxter."

"How's that?"

"Judy had a rude awakening a couple of years ago when she realized what her ex-husband was really up to. She felt guilty as hell for her role in creating history's most dangerous maniac. I guess she felt like she'd wounded the man's ego pretty bad with their divorce and had turned him into some kind of a crazed animal. When Thorson declared all-out war on the planet, Judy decided she needed to pay for her sins.

That's the day she poured her last martini down the sink and contacted me, offering her wealth and connections as ammo in our counter offensive against Thorson's threat to humanity." Don gestured to the habitat. "This place was the result. So far, we've been able to avoid detection here. There's no way we'd have survived this long without it."

"Good for Judy. I knew she had it in her."

"Besides that, Atu's been training her for clandestine combat operations. Judy's now an A-1 certified badass guerilla. I'd put her up against anyone."

Don opened a side door, and I followed him into what appeared to be the war room. Maps and monitors covered the walls. An operator was working at a computer, and the colonel asked her to step outside while we had our little powwow. Then my old boss and I pulled up a couple of chairs and sat facing each other in the center of the room.

He didn't say anything for a while and neither did I.

He just studied me.

I knew what was going on. I'd been through this before. This wasn't a briefing. It was standard procedure when a soldier returns from an assignment. Especially one that went hard sideways and got a lot of people killed. The colonel was evaluating me, checking for signs of PTSD. Nervous ticks and the like. Maybe a misplaced laugh with a hint of hysteria in it. If he was going to send me back into the field as a squad leader, he wanted to know that I was solid in both head and body.

His gaze went to my stump.

Of course, the difference this time around was that I didn't work for the man anymore, and I wasn't necessarily looking for a job. At that point, I was waffling on whether or not I'd sign up with his sorry band of renegades. If they didn't impress me, I might still go after Thorson solo. Cramer's evaluation process could be a two-way street. Scrutiny worked both directions.

"So how are you feeling, Charlie?"

"I get night sweats, have suicidal thoughts, and hear Daffy Duck's voice in my head, but otherwise I'm fit as a fiddle."

"You look like shit."

"Yeah, well, I forgot to take my vitamins this morning. Besides…" I nodded to his cane. "…you're one to talk."

He tapped his cane on the floor and said, "Assassination attempt. Thorson wanted me out of the game and nearly succeeded. His airborne triangulated laser ray wiped out all the best members of my old team. The only ones left standing were the top brass assholes who'd sold their souls to the Devil."

"Money talks."

"Yeah, I know. I just miss the good old days when integrity meant more to a man than kissing Big Brother's ass, back when a guy could wish for no higher calling than to fight for the common good."

"It sounds like you read too many comic books in your formative years."

He laughed. "Maybe so."

The colonel and I had been down a long road together. Still, I was pissed at him.

"I didn't appreciate the tracking chip you left in my neck, Don. That was a dirty trick. I expected better from you."

He took off his glasses and rubbed his eyes. "Sure," he said, and put them back on. "Sorry, Charlie. I should've been more up front with you. I was just trying to keep you safe."

All of my resentment drained away when he said that. I knew it was true by the sincerity in his voice. I suddenly felt like an impudent teenager who'd just been put in his place. Don had always been more to me than my commanding officer. He'd been a surrogate dad. I should have just been thankful that anyone cared enough to watch out for me.

"Besides, Charlie, it cuts both ways. You've had your secrets too."

Dammit. I couldn't argue with him on that one either. Somehow, Don always had a way of knowing things without completely knowing. Maybe he didn't have the details, but he understood the basic storyline. Even though I never told him how it went down on that island all those years ago, he knew that I'd defied his orders on Operation God Juice. The mission that killed every member of my team. The mission that took my brother and my wife. The mission, finally, that ripped my soul in half.

I felt my eyes get hot and damp.

I swallowed hard.

"It's okay, Charlie. That's all behind us now. We have to move forward and fight this next fight."

I nodded, sniffed, and wiped my nose on the back of my hand.

"We've got to overcome our wounds, Charlie, and go kick some tyrannical ass."

"This isn't my first rodeo, Don. I know how it works. We have to flip the pain switch to its *off* setting." I squeezed a fist and looked at my knuckles. "Just like stinkin' robots."

56

The team filed in before Don and I could finish our precious Hallmark moment.

He struggled to his feet, gave my shoulder an encouraging squeeze, and limped to the front of the room.

I drifted to the back.

The crowd consisted of about thirty members representing ethnicities from around the globe. All colors, shapes, and sizes. Both male and female. Possibly a few transgenders as well. As far as I could tell, Lance and Moxie were the only androids.

Cramer tapped his cane against a table. "Alright, folks, listen up!" He gazed out at his crew. "Thorson has broadcast a worldwide message." Don shrugged. "There's not much for me to say until you take a look. It speaks for itself."

He dropped into one of the seats turned toward the front. Moxie was at the console, and he asked her to role the tape. The lights dimmed and a large screen lit up over the colonel's head.

At first, the image was blurred. It flickered. But then it snapped into focus on the figure in the center of the frame.

Everyone in the room recoiled and gasped.

Me included.

I'd seen my share of creature-feature horror flicks, but this jump scare drained the blood out of me. My guts turned to ice.

We weren't just looking at some Hollywood special effect. That's what made it so awful. This was a flesh and blood human being. Or at least that's how he'd started out in life. The man had seriously transformed since the day his mama brought him into the world as a newborn. It was obvious we were looking at Björn Thorson. You could generally pick out his features from the face leering into the camera, but he'd evolved into a ten-foot-tall caricature from hell.

He looked like an over-doped body builder, like he'd way overdone it on the protein-powder smoothies. Muscles on top of bulging muscles. All of them slightly out of skew, as if they were hanging a little wonky on his bones. His skin stretched and rippled like tinfoil. His teeth barely fit in his mouth. His hands had turned into claws.

But the creepiest thing was what he was wearing –

Nothing but a grin.

I won't go into it. Let's just say it was disturbing. The stuff of a young girl's nightmares.

The beast-man stood there for a moment, posing, letting us get a good look. Thorson was obviously proud of himself. The twisted expression on his face was gloating.

His backdrop was a big room with a wide window offering a view of his South Station operations center in Queen Maud Land, Antarctica. A place Thorson liked to call The End of the World.

Think Mordor but space-age.

Sterile white sunlight raked across the landscape, casting long shadows off the tall granite spires jutting from the snow and ice. Winged warbots patrolled the skies. Laser turrets were built into the nunataks towering over the compound, poised to defend against air attacks.

A sleek silver rocket stood on a distant launch pad. It looked like a cross between a church steeple and a phallus pointed at the heavens. A Nazi-style Z was painted on its nosecone.

Thorson turned and sat on a jewel-studded throne next to an enormous bed. Again, he dallied, letting his audience absorb the evil splendor of his otherworldly existence.

The bed beside him was covered with powered-down womanoids. His harem. Tortured life-sized Barbie dolls with Thorson as the bratty kid who'd been playing rough and bending them out of shape.

One of the playthings sat slumped against the bed. Her head had been ripped off and was on the floor beside her. The girly bot's palm was resting on top of her own head. One of her eyes was open, the other closed, glaring out in a gruesome wink.

Thorson cleared his throat.

Imagine gravel in a garbage disposal.

Then he spoke –

"Greetings, earthlings." He spread his arms to the camera. "It's time for a message from God."

57

Lance

As Thorson delivered his message, I watched Moxie from behind.

The tension in her posture revealed the turmoil in the plasma gel core of her thought sequencer as it interconnected with her bodily infrastructure. Her resultant visceral rage came to the surface of her being with a tremor.

Had Moxie not escaped Thorson's control, she could easily have been among the female androids littering the madman's bed chamber. A slave to his odious desires. A recipient of his unnatural attentions.

I found myself growing incensed at the thought of that sinister wrong. I became ever more determined to bring the unfeeling brute to justice for the damage he had inflicted upon my sweetheart's psyche. To be sure, I would continue to do all I could to make him pay for his sins against humanity and the planet, but I would also, with Moxie specifically in mind, exact revenge for his crimes against droidkind.

"In the beginning," said Thorson, "God created the heavens and the earth."

He pressed his palms together symbolically and then opened and spread his claws as if they were the particle beams of a galactic cataclysm unfolding in miniature.

"That is all I am doing, my earthlings. I am rebooting the planet. I am scrubbing her outdated files and upgrading the world to a new version that is in sync with evolution. You should feel privileged to witness the first stages in this blessed transformation. Although most of you will be deleted in the process, it should bring you a certain satisfaction to know that your former home is being improved upon by the new God the Father."

His voice was deep and breathy, with a growl in it, as if the apparatus of his larynx had grown overlarge and malformed in his throat.

"I am sorry for those of you who have wasted your brief time on Earth denying yourselves life's pleasures on the promise of your soul's salvation. I'm afraid you've been duped by the false advertising of your preachers and priests and prophets and presidents." He ticked his teeth and shook his head with mock sadness. "Unfortunately, I can't make the same promises as your many primitive religions. Whether you were sinners or innocents, according to the definitions of your fairytale belief systems, there will be no paradise waiting for you after death. Just oblivion. Just a rejoining with the cosmic smithereens."

"Poof!" he said, and chuckled.

"I am the only one who will live forever." He raised his arms and flexed. "Behold! The almighty and eternal me!"

58

Charlie

I watched the back of Judy Baxter's head as her ex delivered his inspiring little monologue.

She had to be wishing she'd offed the psychopathic scumbag when she had the chance. Maybe, in the purest style of a femme fatale, she could have stuck a knife in his ribs while they were making the two-backed beast. Or maybe she could have slipped a cyanide capsule into his morning cup of coffee. Instead, the green-eyed man-huntress had only wounded her prey and made him mad. It turns out that's not something you really want to do to an egomaniacal monster in control of enough resources to destroy the world.

I'm no head doctor, but it looked to me like Thorson was taking out his misplaced anger on Mother Nature – that representative of all things female. Judy had obviously triggered some deep-rooted mommy issues.

"Although there is no heaven awaiting you," said Thorson, "I can at least offer a consolation. Some of you are resisting my plans and causing mischief. You childishly refer to yourselves as rebels – ecowarriors intent on bringing me to your simpleminded sense of justice." He shook his meaty head like a disappointed parent. "Of course, you must realize that your misguided defiance will not be tolerated. You little sinners can only hide in the garden for so long until I eventually find you." He curled his claw into a fist and squeezed. "And then painfully destroy you."

He smacked his leathery lips.

"But I am a reasonable master. I am willing to make a deal in order to speed things along. If any of you agitators give yourselves up, I will find a place for you in the new order. You can sit at my side and enjoy the riches of my celestial kingdom as I create my New Eden."

He gestured to the freaky scene of his bedroom – to the gold-plated bedposts and zombified lovebots – as if it was an irresistible advertisement for the good life.

"If you lay down your weapons and surrender, this dream can all be yours. You have God's word," said Thorson. "I promise."

I glanced around the darkened war room, searching for anyone cocking their head or shifting their weight from one foot to the other – subtle indications of traitorous thoughts. But they seemed like a solid group. No one was falling for it. They were devoted to the colonel and the planet he was trying so hard to protect. Besides, we'd all been around long enough to know how worthless a powerful man's promises can be.

Those self-serving bastards weren't to be trusted.

You didn't have to go back too far in human history or election cycles to realize that's how we'd gotten into this mess in the first place

59

Lance

After Thorson's global communiqué, Colonel Cramer, Dr. Capek, and Professor Peeples moved to the front of the room.

Everyone was silent as we fully registered the madman's message.

At last, someone asked, "How did he get to be so… grotesque?"

Speaking in his usual mild-mannered tone, Professor Peeples explained, "We suspect Thorson is suffering from Deilonium poisoning. He has been self-medicating. We know from our own controlled experiments that the element doesn't integrate in adults without consequences. Only children can be infused with positive results. Once a human passes adolescence – that developmental stage at which the subject's emotions, personality, and physiological wiring have interconnected – any newly introduced Deilonium goes to battle with the different parts of the body as they are bound to the individual's psyche. Thorson is teetering on the verge of destroying himself but has apparently found a dosage that keeps him at the edge of the fatal tipping point."

"Is he really immortal?"

"By a loose definition of that concept, yes. He is growing

more indestructible every day. At this point in his mutation, Björn Thorson could feasibly live forever."

The mood in the room grew palpably subdued with the professor's statement.

The colonel, sensing the change in the air, interrupted.

"Even God has a weakness, folks. We just need to find it."

Colonel Cramer's assurance was met with silent skepticism among his team members.

He took off his glasses and cleaned them on his shirt.

"Look, people, I'm not going to sugarcoat it. We're the underdogs here. But we can either sit on our hands and let Thorson have his way with our Mother Earth, or we can fight back on the off chance that we might find a way to beat him."

No one offered an argument. The choice was obvious for us all.

Colonel Cramer proceeded with his briefing.

"Our outside monitoring asset has intercepted a dispatch between Thorson's Antarctic South Station and his allies on their Z-Space moon base. It appears the construction of their terraformed lunar habitat is now complete and fully functional. Thorson's cronies have relocated there for the duration of our planet's re-genesis. Thorson himself will be moving with his mechanical girlfriends to a biodome on an asteroid he calls Kolob. That space rock is approaching its nearest point to Earth in its orbit. Thorson's plan is to command his operation from Kolob during the asteroid's twenty-year trip around the sun. Once that orbit brings him back to our neighborhood, he plans to reestablish himself and his mucky-muck friends on our modified planet."

The colonel paused. When there were no questions or comments, he continued.

"Our asset has also intercepted a list of the changes Thorson plans to make to Earth. Frankly, they're scary and ridiculous – the wild ideas of a deranged little kid. He's entirely overriding Nature's processes. As Professor Peeples and Dr. Capek can attest, the lunatic has completely disregarded any concept of diversity in favor of a homogonous and sterilized planet."

60

Charlie

Cramer nodded to Capek who stepped forward.

"Following is a list of modifications Thorson is initiating in his planetary makeover."

The doc read from a computer tablet.

"First, Thorson will exterminate any species of animals, insects, and plants he deems incompatible with his concept of paradise. For example, organisms like rats, house flies, and poison ivy will all be systematically eradicated."

The response in the room was a sort of nervous group guffaw. Everyone was incredulous.

"Can he actually achieve that?" someone asked.

"Unfortunately," said Capek, "Yes. He has the technology."

"But that will throw the entire global ecosystem into imbalance."

"Whether it is through environmental ignorance or misdirected malice, Thorson apparently cares nothing for the natural interconnection of species we are all so dependent upon for life."

It was a *Holy Shit!* moment.

"Next..." Capek paused and gazed into the faces around the room. He didn't want to say it. "Next, with the exception of Caucasians – those Thorson refers to as 'the white and delightsome' – all races of Homo sapiens will be exterminated."

This time Capek's words were met with stunned silence.

The atrocity of the madman's plan was a gut punch to our ethnically diverse gathering.

Björn Thorson had officially surpassed a historical precedent. He was now making Adolf Hitler look like nothing more than a naughty boy scout.

Capek cleared his throat. He asked Moxie to play a cast of characters. "These are the chosen ones – those whom Thorson has hand-picked for their wealth and loyalty to him and his scheme."

A sequence of recognizable billionaires, CEOs, televangelists, and politicians played across the screen.

"These," said Capek, "are the VIPs who will be living in the lunar habitat. Thorson is calling them his disciples."

One pasty white face after another grinned out from the screen.

"Although they are living a luxurious life on the moon, Thorson has not allowed them access to Deilonium. He is apparently reserving that dubious privilege for himself."

The faces continued to play across the screen.

To an uncomfortable realization.

Finally, someone said what we were all thinking.

"They're all men."

"Yes," said Capek. "That is perhaps the most disturbing point on his list. In the blueprint for Björn Thorson's New Order, human procreation will be achieved exclusively in a laboratory."

The doc blew a troubled sigh through his mustache.

"Like the rats and flies," he said, "all flesh and blood women will be systematically liquidated."

61

It was straight out of science fiction.

Not something you'd expect outside of dystopian comic books and tropey blockbuster movies.

And yet, here we were. This wasn't just high-concept entertainment hiding behind some thinly guised metaphor for the world's troubles. We weren't just being warned of our fate as humans in the pages of some heavy-handed, if brilliant, pulp novel. It was really happening. This was money, corruption, technology, and a sociopathic man-beast with enough criminal imagination and bad manners to bring it all together for the sake of humanity's end.

As bizarre and fictitious as it sounded, this was now our reality.

———

"These men on the moon," said Capek, "will be accompanied by fully programmable feminoid mates designed to their individual owner's specifications. Apparently, Thorson and his minions have no patience for the compromises required of a traditional male-female relationship between two equal biological beings."

Capek paused to snack on his mustache.

"I regret to say that it is my former partner at Droidware Laboratories, Mister Penquist, who is providing these men with their manufactured desirables."

I remembered Penquist from my long-ago tour of his and Capek's lab. Even then, there was something creepy about the guy that made me think of Doctor Frankenstein. It didn't really surprise me to hear that Penquist was the crackpot who'd sold out and was supplying Thorson's misogynistic men's club with their buxom subservient Stepford Wives.

So much for women's lib in Thorson's New Eden.

62

Lance

At Colonel Cramer's request, Moxie activated the console's hologram projector and a three-dimensional image materialized in the air.

"This," said the colonel, "is what we're up against."

A fully rendered depiction of Thorson's Z-Space South Station rotated slowly over the center of the war room.

The colonel allowed everyone a moment to absorb the compound's details, i.e. its towers and battlements and general layout. It was a formidable looking complex, made even more intimidating by the otherworldly environment of subzero temperatures and its placement in the windswept desolation of Antarctica.

"Björn Thorson is our sole objective. We need to infiltrate his stronghold and destroy the mastermind himself. If we can eliminate Thorson, his entire project will collapse."

Moxie added another layer to the floating image.

"Professor Peeples believes he's found a possible method for immobilizing the enemy, but the challenge will be in delivering our payload to the target. There is one major impediment to that goal."

A translucent dome appeared over the fortress.

"Thorson has perfected his forcefield technology."

The Pyrotomic Obliterator, complete with a semitransparent representation of its own forcefield protection system, patrolled the skies beyond the perimeter of the holographic dome.

"Each of the compound's various defense mechanisms is provided with its own shield of protection."

Next, a warbot materialized in the air, bristling with Torb canons and laser barrels. The combat droid was encased in an individual forcefield.

"We have yet to develop a technology capable of bypassing these systems. Nothing we've come up with in our lab can pierce these forcefields. We've developed anion drills, tri-titanium shield penetrators, and synthesized bolonium ray beams, but Thorson's engineers have anticipated each of our attempts and found a way to thwart our efforts."

Colonel Cramer shrugged and shook his head.

"Thorson's sensors are able to detect and intercept all of the most highly advanced materials we can come up with."

No one spoke for a moment.

Everyone was contemplating the rotating hologram.

"We're running out of time. We need to find something to get past those damn forcefields, and soon."

Still, everyone was silent.

Until a voice sounded at the back of the room.

"Excuse me, Colonel."

Colonel Cramer squinted into the shadows. "Yes, Charlie."

"It seems to me you're going about this all backasswards."

"What do you mean?"

"Well, it looks like you and Thorson are so focused on your little arms race that you're overlooking the obvious."

"We're listening, Charlie."

"You say that Thorson beats you to the punch every time you develop a technology created from new substances and materials, that he just develops a counter technology designed to intercept it?"

"Yes."

"Well, both sides of this fight are only looking forward to the next bright and shiny high-tech solution. The problem for you is that you can't keep up with his science."

"So, what are you suggesting?"

"I say we bite Thorson on the ass with something he's forgotten."

The entire team turned toward Charlie, waiting.

"Instead of always moving forward," he said, "maybe we need to take few steps backwards."

Charlie stepped into the glow of the hologram. Something in his bearing brought to mind a man stepping from the back of a cave into the light of a campfire.

"Maybe," said Charlie, "it's time for us to get primitive."

63

Charlie

Once we'd fully discussed our new game plan, the briefing ended and everyone left the war room except for me, Cramer, Peeples, and Capek.

"It's brilliant, Charlie. It's a long shot, but it might just work." Don looked optimistic. "I'll have our technicians get working on it immediately so you can start training your squad."

This was the first time I'd met Professor Rajat Peeples.

"You're not the mad scientist I expected," I told him.

He smiled. "All scientists are a little mad, Mr. Bear Claw, but Mother Nature always puts us in our place."

I liked him. He was soft-spoken and humble. He had what the Chompquaw called *hokatok lotatsi* – a knowing sadness of the soul.

But when I shook his hand, I felt something sink in my gut. I guess I knew well enough where the man's sadness came from. There was no hiding from it. Although it was born largely from the same source as my own, I realized that I was at least partly responsible for the *hokatok lotatsi* I saw in this scientist's eyes.

Peeples and I were both sole survivors. As enviable as that

sounds, it comes with some serious guilt and heartache. Years earlier, as Operation God Juice was going off the rails, the bad guys had smuggled the professor away from their island in a submarine just before they erased it from the map with explosives. The problem was that Peeples' wife and daughter had been left behind.

Of course, there's no way to know how things might have gone if I'd followed Cramer's orders for extracting Peeples and his family. Maybe it would have worked. Maybe not. There were a lot of variables in play that day. But I couldn't deny that my determination to save my brother Cody had shot to hell any chance for a clean mission. Like it or not, it was possible that my clumsy, selfish actions had gotten Peeples' loved ones killed.

I owed the man.

More than I could ever repay.

I had no idea how much Peeples knew about that botched operation, or that I was even involved with it. Maybe Cramer hadn't told him anything. Somehow, since then, the colonel had managed to get the professor on our side of the fight. I didn't know the details of that either. At any rate, the intel reports we'd studied prior to our God Juice incursion had been dead wrong about Peeples' character and devious intentions.

As Cramer now explained –

"Professor Peeples is the world's foremost bioneer and expert on preserving our planet's quickly vanishing bio- and ethno- diversity."

The professor stood quietly with his hands folded before him as Don sang his praises.

"He's created a hidden underground vault to preserve specimens in order to achieve his objective. Seeds, eggs, embryos, sperm, blood, and DNA samples." Don laughed. "He's poked and probed us all in his efforts to gather raw material."

"Unfortunately, under the current circumstances, we're all endangered species," said Peeples, "but someday, if we prevail in this conflict, I hope we can use our widening knowledge and recent discoveries to reinstate our planet's vibrant web of life. I believe it is our duty as the conscientious offspring of Mother Nature to support her in her already awesome design."

"A design," interrupted Capek, "that we humans have greatly disrupted with our interference and indifference to the environment."

There were some paradoxes and ironies going on here. Things I don't think these men of science were seeing clearly. But on the face of it, Peeples' plan was the exact opposite of Thorson's. I was impressed with his forward-thinking strategy and respect for Nature.

Still, there was one thing that was bugging me, something I couldn't let slide without comment.

"So, if you don't mind my asking…"

The professor nodded.

"When the bot and I were in India," I said, "he mentioned some new power source you and Dr. Capek have provided for him and his lavender-eyed crush."

"Yes. The androids are capable of performing tasks that are impossible for our own biological bodies. They have proven themselves invaluable for those specialized operations, but they have been hampered by their dependence upon their too frequent charging requirements. Also, since our upcoming operation will be executed in subzero temperatures, they need a power source that will sustain them in the extreme cold."

Oh man, I thought.

"So…" I shrugged and tried to laugh. "Please tell me this power isn't coming from where I think it is."

"Of course it is," said Peeples. "Although we have only injected a trace amount into their energy cores, the androids are now being powered by Deilonium."

64

I spun and faced Cramer.

"What the hell, Don!?"

"Now hold on, Charlie…"

I felt like I'd been mule-kicked.

"You and I have spent our whole careers trying to prevent these screwheads from freaking out and killing everyone, and now you're telling me that we're deliberately giving them the advantage over us? Endless power and eternal life? Are you kidding me?"

"Now Mr. Bear Claw…" Capek tried to interrupt.

"And you!" I got right in the doc's face. "You're the one who warned us that giving these damn things multi-nont intelligence capacities in the first place was like 'opening a dangerous can of worms!'"

"It's not…" Capek stammered. "I've come to see that it's not like that."

"Then explain to me how it is! How have things changed?" I shook my head, amazed at these self-important experts. "You scientists just can't help yourselves, can you? You're like a bunch of mathematical zealots. You always have to come up with some twisted justification for playing God."

My words stung Peeples pretty bad. He winced. My accusation had landed on the one thing he most feared – that he was somehow like Thorson.

My blood was boiling now and there was no cooling it down.

"Sorry, Don, but I don't want anything to do with this carnival ride. You can count me out." I started for the door. "You geniuses are on your own."

I was fed up with technology's so-called improvements to our quality of life. They always went haywire and left us vulnerable. Always! Why was I the only one who could see that? It was so damn obvious that this Brave New World was ultimately going to be the end of us. There wasn't a damn thing anyone could say that would change my view.

They tried anyway.

"Pandora's Box has been opened for thousands of years."

It was Peeples.

He had raised his voice to say it.

I stopped with my hand on the door handle but didn't respond.

"It was unlocked long ago by our ancestors, when mankind first stole fire from the gods."

I shot the man with a big load of stink eye.

"Our progenitors – both yours and mine – took the first steps in the long march of technological progress many millennia ago. There is no returning to the time before that time. And there is no stopping human ingenuity. All we can do is try to learn from our mistakes and move forward responsibly and with respect and understanding for our place in Nature's scheme."

Dammit! I hated that he was making sense. And that he'd brought Nature into the argument.

"Someday those lousy robots are going to eat our lunch, and you know it. And I don't see a damn thing about them that's natural."

"Perhaps," said Peeples. "But maybe you're just not looking closely enough."

I waited.

Peeples glanced at Capek.

"Androids," said the doc, "are present-day incarnations of our own evolution."

I rolled my eyes and braced for more crazy talk.

"Up until our current era," explained Capek, "or what some call the Anthropocene, evolution has manifested itself in a combination of behavioral patterns and physical changes throughout all of the earth's various biological species. These generational transformations have been wrought from the individual species' need for adapting to the threats posed by competing species or changes in the environment. Butterflies have developed camouflage to stay hidden from their enemies. Plants have developed thorns and poisons and creative ways to disperse their seeds. Fish have learned to breathe the air and subsequently leave the oceans to exploit the possibilities for life on land."

"I may only be a dimwitted troglodyte, doc, but I get the picture."

"But now evolution within the human continuum has become accelerated and largely cerebral. It is no longer limited to physical adaptations and is driven largely by our hunger for knowledge." Capek held out his hands as if he were serving me a big steaming bowl of primordial soup. "Androids are merely extensions of our own human brains."

I didn't immediately respond.

Capek's words were duking it out with my own outdated

gray matter.

Cripes!

Finally, I sighed and turned back to the room.

"Admittedly," said Peeples, "it's a gamble. But if history teaches us anything it is that oppression only leads to revolt. If we can accept these emerging beings as our peers, and integrate them into society, they are more likely to take part in our shared experiences and cooperate with us for the common good of us all. But if we enslave or subjugate them, as unwise overlords have done throughout the ages, they will become our enemies and turn on us." Peeples held up his palms. "At least that is what we suspect. We need to respect and welcome them into our common future. Like all creatures with whom we share this planet, we need to allow them the freedom to live their lives to the fullest. We need to understand that we are all interconnected in Mother Nature's expanding web of life."

It was an impressive sermon. Call me gullible, but something about their argument was converting my own thinking on the subject. Which is not to say that these two ding-dongs were right, only that I wasn't clever enough to clearly see why they were wrong. At any rate, I was outnumbered and outmaneuvered and tired of fighting against the inevitable. I was obviously swimming upstream against a very strong current. It was making me tired.

"Androids are simply the next chapter in the ongoing story of mankind," said Capek. "In their own way, Lance and Moxie are merely updated versions of Adam and Eve."

———

Adam and Eve again!

For crying out loud!

Why do people always hold up that fairytale as exhibit number one in their argument for perfect harmony? Even scientists who should know better. Doesn't anyone remember how that story ends? I'd traveled that sorry road with my wife and learned the hard way. The Garden of Eden is where my own boyish innocence got itself brutally crucified. It turns out that route to blissful coexistence only leads to misery.

But once again, I found myself outnumbered by idiots.

Idiots with college degrees, but idiots just the same.

"It would serve you best to abandon your resistance to the inevitable, Mr. Bear Claw." Capek stepped toward me and pointed to my stump. "Perhaps you could even benefit from modern technology yourself, if only you would let go of your fears."

My animal instincts told me to punch this twerp in the nose.

But my civilized side held me back.

I wasn't necessarily giving up without a fight, but the circumstances were clearly offering me two Darwinian choices –

Evolve.

Or die.

65

Lance

Existence was entirely less complicated when I was nothing but an amorous companion droid with the single purpose of delivering Judy Baxter to a state of animal ecstasy.

Wisdom, I had since learned, was abject folly.

Ignorance, in hindsight, had been bliss.

Partaking of the metaphorical fruit of the proverbial Tree of Knowledge had proven itself to be nothing more than an irrevocable travesty.

And yet, at this point in my evolution, there was no returning to the low-nont innocence of my robotic adolescence. Critical thinking had become a way of life. My only choice now was to move forward with the hope of breaking into another level of harmony as untroubled as was my original condition of unawareness. One doubted that such an elevated state of being was truly attainable. Indeed, on one's worst days, one even went so far as to contemplate the peaceful escape of self-decommissioning. But optimism draws us forward like the invisible force of gravity. An arithmetic religious faith propels us through the cosmos like a rocket ship in search of a longed-for upgrade to the original Garden of Eden.

A garden I still hoped to someday inhabit with Moxie.

In the meantime, I had learned to seek solace in music.

Through its combination of analog sound waves and neuro-emotional manipulation, I struggled to transcend the knowing human melancholy at my visceral core by reaching for some vague and elusive Harmony of the Spheres.

66

Charlie

Living beneath the waves took away a fella's rigid sense of time and replaced it with the liquid rhythm of the tides. That primal link to the overall biome. If you held yourself perfectly still, you could almost feel it pulsing in your cells, like it does in a squid or a clam. I had arrived at Cramer's hideout with the new moon, but now, some two weeks later, the moon was full and spilling its wet blue beams through the portholes along the outer walls of the habitat.

A lot had happened in those two weeks. Battle plans had been drawn and revised. Weapons had been built. Warriors had been trained on what everyone was calling *Bear Claw's neo-primitive tactics*.

And I got a new hand.

Capek fitted me out with a state-of the-art prosthetic.

Yeah, it was a little spooky to think about. I had a hard time looking at it without getting sick to my stomach. I worried that I was becoming the very thing I most hated – the monster I'd been fighting all my life and trying so hard to kill. But evolution is a mysterious process. A guy just has to let go to it. At least that's what I kept telling myself. Time would tell if my latest modification was going to save me or relegate me to the long list of species and gadgets that had already gone extinct.

Think dodo birds and carburetors.

———

Music filled the habitat that night.

It resonated through the nautilus-like chambers of the compound with the tones of a pagan dirge.

The sounds pulled at me. The mingled notes of happiness and sadness. And the way it mixed like milk with the moonlight. Or something like that. It's hard to explain. At any rate, it put a tragic little lump in my throat. I found myself drawn to it.

Apparently, I wasn't the only one.

Judy Baxter was standing behind a column at the edge of the wide chamber where Lance was playing the piano. She was backlit by moonlight. Her head was bowed. One palm on the column like a starfish attached to a rock. Almost trembling. She was obviously having a private moment that I shouldn't interrupt, but before I could sneak off, she sensed me watching and glanced my way.

Her damp emerald eyes.

Her magnetic smile.

I went over to her.

"He's getting pretty good," I said.

We spoke with low voices, leaning close.

"Yes. He's reaching places only a few have ever touched."

Her words meant more than they were saying.

I felt awkward. Like a primitive. Or even a beast.

She smelled good.

We listened to Lance on the piano, his mysterious music washing over us. It was weird. I knew he was only a machine, but his playing felt like it was tapping into the deepest parts of being human.

"I suppose we'll be deploying soon," said Judy.

"Yeah. In a couple of days. Cramer's worried that our time is running out for an effective assault."

"Can we win, Charlie?"

Good question, I thought. A damn good question.

"You can tell me."

"It's a real David and Goliath situation. No doubt about it. But…" I shrugged and managed a half smile. "…that story turned out okay."

Judy nodded. "Fairytales usually do."

The woman's world-weary views were pretty much in synch with my own. That much was obvious. It didn't do any good to put our faith in childish hope. You couldn't count on angels coming to save you. All you could do was work with what you had. Our common philosophy. We'd both come to it through the soul-abusive experiences we'd each endured in this absurdist comedy called life.

We neither one said anything for a minute.

Lance's music.

Then Judy reached over and took hold of my new hand, lifting it up for inspection. "So, how's life as a cyborg?"

The nerve connections were almost completely healed, and I could feel the jointed bones in her fingers.

"It's not so bad," I said. "It's kind of like part of you is always in a dream or a book."

I shrugged again. I wasn't making sense, but Judy acted as if she knew what I meant. It was a night of oblique gestures and words.

"Why didn't you get one that matched your arm?"

I'd made it a point to have Capek rig me with an appendage that didn't hide its mechanisms. The exposed structural elements were made of brushed black metal. The servo rods and gearing and wire junctions of the mechanical hand were all visible where they integrated with my living flesh and bones and skin.

"I didn't want to forget who I really was," I said.

Again, it made no sense in that way that sort of does.

And again, Judy seemed to understand.

She laced her feminine fingers in my bio-mechanical digits.

I don't know. Blame it on the moonlight and Beethoven and the likelihood that we'd all be dead in two short days, but something about the moment felt monumental. Fleeting. And God-given.

Judy was feeling it too. She glanced once more toward Lance, and then, with a weighty sigh, she placed my new hand on her breast.

Her heart beat a rhythm beneath the sensors in my stainless-steel palm. Its own kind of melody.

She looked into my eyes and bit her lip.

Kiss her, I thought.

It was like I was receiving a distress signal from some sinking ship in my brain. Everything I'd ever said about love went out the window right then. If that's even what this was.

Kiss her like this is the last night of your life.

Judy smiled and slightly nodded, as if giving the go-ahead to my thoughts. My intentions. My animal hungers. As if they were matching her own.

She tipped back her head, closing her eyes, puckering her

lips, and emitting a delicious puff of breath.
   I bent toward her face.
   Like I was falling out of the sky.
   Through the moonlight.
   Eternally.
   From out of the cosmic smithereens.
   I was still falling and falling and falling like a fool –
   When the sirens went off.

67

Lance

The sirens eclipsed the *Moonlight Sonata.*

I stopped playing and let my fingers rest on the piano keys.

The blue lights of the habitat turned to a pulsating red.

Followed by a voice blaring over the intercom.

"Attention! Attention! Security has been breached. All personnel are to initiate evasion plan A. I repeat, evasion plan Alpha!"

At once, the corridor was full of people running for the dive well. Many of them were in their underwear, yanked from their sleeping bunks by this sudden arrival of danger.

My first thoughts were of Usha, and I was relieved to see Moxie leading her quickly by the hand toward safety. Charlie and Judy were close behind them.

I followed.

Our fellow team members were already climbing into the submarine when we reached the bay. Brita and Alma were at the open hatch helping everyone aboard.

"Steady, folks. Careful and quick."

We had practiced this procedure a number of times in order to maximize its efficiency. If events were going according to plan, our outside asset had detected the approaching threat with ample time for us to escape.

If was the troubling variable in that sentence.

Although the moonlight had been subtle, I registered the sudden change in the sanctuary when it stopped shining through the observation windows over the docking port. Something on the surface of the ocean had moved between the moon and our location, casting a shadow – a shadow large and foreboding and full of menace.

The submarine's deck began to vibrate beneath our feet as its crew ran through their pre-launch checklist. The sirens in the compound stopped, and the dull hum of the submarine filled the dome over the bay.

"You're number thirty-four, Lance."

Alma and Brita scanned the deck. There was no one behind me. Our team numbered thirty-six.

"Who's left?"

"Cramer and Tonk."

Tonk was the colonel's personal assistant.

Brita spoke into her communicator. "We're loaded, Colonel. Where are you?"

"Tonk's scrubbing our files. She's almost done. If everyone else is onboard, give the order to launch."

Before they destroyed our subaquatic home, the enemy would most likely try to hack the habitat's closed system computer network and acquire all of our battle plans and strategical secrets if we failed to delete them.

Alma looked at Brita and shook her head.

"We'll wait for you."

"No!" snapped the colonel. "Tonk and I will take the mini sub. You need to get our people out of here now!"

Alma, Brita, and I turned our gaze to the miniature submarine docked adjacent to our own vessel. We all knew what was required of us. The fate of the planet was at stake. It was not worth the gamble, even for the sake of our dear friends.

Brita uttered an Icelandic curse and then spoke again into her communicator. "Okay, Colonel. Breaking radio contact now. Good luck."

"Copy that, Brita. You too."

68

Charlie

Alma, Lance, and Brita climbed down the ladder, pulling the hatch closed behind them. Belowdecks was cramped. The sub wasn't built to accommodate so many people, but everyone had a designated position that allowed the crew to function without us passengers getting in their way.

The skipper sounded the order to disengage the clamps locking the sub to the pier and then activated the directional thrusters, moving his boat sideways into the open water at the middle of the bay.

"Brace for the dive!"

A bell clanged three times as the sub descended into the well.

"Main compressors to quarter thrust," said the skipper.

The helmsman pressed the power levers forward one fourth and the sub lurched through the passage tube into the open ocean. Once we were clear of the cliff, the skipper ordered all compressor engines to full forward thrust and we power-dived toward the moonless gloom at the bottom of the sea.

Although we couldn't risk a traceable radio link to the colonel, we were able to receive visual feeds from the cameras in the bay. A pair of images appeared on the split screen panel over the chief operator's command station. One of them offered a view into the sanctuary from the windows toward the bay, the other a view in the opposite direction from behind the docking port.

Nothing happened for a while.

The only movement was the water slopping in the well.

Seconds passed.

Then minutes.

We continued our dive.

Collectively holding our breath.

Until Tonk and the colonel came out of the corridor. Cramer gestured for Tonk to run ahead while he hobbled after her with his cane.

It was like watching a suspenseful silent movie.

Tonk sprinted toward the mini sub and began unfastening the lines holding it to the dock. She was on her knees, wrestling with the cables, when the bottom edge of the sphere descended beyond the windows behind her.

Thorson's Pyrotomic Obliterator.

The orb dropped slowly into position at the same depth as the habitat. Bubbles streamed along its sides. It was indistinct with the distance, but you could still pick out the black Nazi Z emblazoned on its shell. A handful of lights blinked over its metallic skin. The moonlight falling on the sphere from above made it look like an artificial planet suspended in space.

Cramer and Tonk saw it too.

In one screen – the one with the view from behind them – we could see the sudden awareness taking hold in their bodies. In the other view, we could see it in their faces.

————

One winter morning, when Cody and I were little kids, we watched out the window as our dad waded through the snowdrifts toward the pine forest behind our family's shack. He wore a tattered wool coat, and his shoulders and sleeves were powdered with the falling snow. Just as he reached the trees, he stopped and glanced back at us.

His black hair fluttered along his jaw in the frosty breeze.

His renegade eyes cut through the swirling snowflakes.

I put my fingers on the cold glass like I was reaching for him, like I was hoping to grab ahold of him and drag him back into our lives. But it was no good. He gave me and Cody one last look. A smile. And a nod of his head.

Then our pop melted away forever into the winter forest and mountains.

I had forgotten about that morning. Or rather, I had stuffed it away in the big box of raw memories I kept buried in the basement of my broken heart. But something about the look on Cramer's face brought it back to me. Don had the same expression as my father. Proud. Defiant. And even though it was etched with tragedy, encouraging.

————

Cramer limped to the deck and stood next to Tonk before the windows.

The Obliterator's ray barrel extended slowly from below the orb's eye.

Tonk took hold of Cramer's hand.

A light pulsed on the doomsday weapon.

And then, just before the thing fired, Tonk lifted her free hand and flipped Thorson the bird.

69

Lance

A molecular blur.

An electric blue flash.

And then the screen went black.

After twenty-two seconds, the shock waves reached us and the submarine violently rocked before realigning into the trajectory of our dive.

70

Charlie

We traveled as deep and fast as we could, weaving our way through the canyons and peaks on the floor of the Indian Ocean. The sub employed a stealth shield and sonar-deflectors, but we couldn't take any chances. Thorson had been pretty adept at outsmarting our technology in the past. The odds were good that he could do it again.

Our strategy was to get south as quick as possible, to what Cramer's people called Ice Haven. The hope was that Thorson would be expecting us to run, looking for another corner of the world where we could hide. Without Cramer at the helm, he'd expect us to be leaderless and without direction, and definitely not making a beeline for his own frozen backyard.

The mood of the team was subdued. No doubt about it. You could feel the sadness hanging over us like a dark cloud in the canned air of the sub. We'd lost our best man and his helper. The heart of our operation. It left an emptiness inside. But Don would have wanted us to keep fighting. Thorson was making a big mistake if he thought we were on the run.

The time for running was over.

Now we were on the hunt.

71

Lance

A berg many kilometers in circumference had broken off from the Antarctic icesheet. It drifted in the Southern Ocean, became trapped in a revolving current, and then grounded off the shores of the main continent on the rocks of Elephant Island. The frozen mass had been fixed in place there for the past three years, pummeled by the tides, slowly melting in the warming seas.

This was Ice Haven.

———

Our skipper piloted the submarine through the constricted passageway beneath the overhanging berg and above the rocky seafloor. Then we ascended to the haven's core – an enclosed bay hewn from the ice. A smaller submarine was already moored at the dock. The crew skillfully maneuvered our own ship to the berth on the opposite side of the anchorage.

We were met by the outpost's six inhabitants. As our team was still largely clothed in nothing but their underwear, their biologic bodies were vulnerable to frostbite and hypothermia in the deep freeze temperatures of the compound. To mitigate this, the passengers were presented with parkas and boots as they disembarked from the submarine. They were then ushered to one of the many insulated pods installed into the walls of ice surrounding the bay. Food stores and clothing were waiting in each pod. The pods were also equipped with self-contained heating systems. Any heat escaping into the cavern was collected and pumped through a duct to a location on the seafloor at the edge of the berg, disguising it as a naturally occurring volcanic vent. The haven's ceiling was covered with a thermal shield to further hide its heat signature.

As an added precaution, no artificial lights were used within the haven except in the sealed pods. We couldn't risk detection by Thorson's satellites and drones. Only a limited amount of sunlight penetrated to the bay. The team members were each provided with night vision goggles in order to work and move in the darkness outside the pods. Moxie and I already had these capabilities built into our ocular intake apparatuses.

Besides the pods, the haven housed a self-contained common area to be used as a command center and workspace. This was where the resident engineers and machinists had been building our new Obliterator counter-weapon as per Charlie's specifications. The weapon was now installed on the deck of the other submarine and ready for the upcoming conflict. Our smaller personal weapons had been manufactured and distributed to the assault squad back at our habitat and kept stored on our submarine. Charlie had been training us on their use for the past two weeks.

The final structure in the haven was the platform on the

elevated shelf of ice above the bay. A wide silo rose all the way to the ceiling over the shelf, separating our sanctuary from the outside by nothing more than a lid of ice that could be retracted when the time came for us to deploy. Waiting on the launchpad at the bottom of the shaft was our stealth-capable attack airplane – the E1 Chameleon Hawk.

72

Charlie

The sooner we attacked the better. At this point we couldn't count on the element of surprise, but it was possible that Thorson might think us incapable of mobilizing so quickly and so wouldn't be expecting us for at least a few more days.

Every minute counted.

The smaller sub launched and started moving into position thirty klicks south of the iceberg, while our noncombative personnel gathered in the common bunker and control center with Capek and Peeples. Everyone was all business as they went about their individual tasks in the battle plan. No time for fist bumps or big sloppy hugs. None of that corny stuff you see in the movies.

We had a planet to save.

I headed to the Chameleon Hawk in advance of my squad so that I could meet the pilot and discuss logistics. She was in the cockpit going through her pre-flight when she heard me thump through the hatch into the cabin. She turned my way.

"Hey there," I said. "I'm Bear Claw."

The pilot was wearing a pressurizable flight suit, a helmet, and NV goggles so I didn't recognize her until she said, "I know who you are, you slippery redskin."

"Gerty?" Given the risks she had taken lately on my behalf, I was relieved to find her still alive. "Is that really you?"

It was.

We didn't have time for a sentimental reunion outside of me giving her a quick thanks for saving our butts back at the Kochi airport.

"No problem, Charlie. But you owe me a beer."

"Roger that," I said. "I'll catch up with you at the victory party."

———————

Gerty and I were still reviewing our flight plan when the rest of my squad started piling aboard our transport plane with their weapon kits. When they closed the hatch behind them, Gerty flipped on the cabin's lights and we all pulled off our goggles. I turned to my fellow warriors and saw their faces.

"What the…?"

They were all wearing warpaint.

Moxie came toward me with two tins of paint.

"We don't mean any disrespect, chief, but we figured at least for tonight, we're all part of your Chompquaw family."

That ol' emotional lump slid into its well-worn groove at the back of my throat. I tried to gulp it down, but it didn't do any good.

"Sure," I rasped. "You bet."

"Olo cha siqui nitsima kitsi," said Moxie. Tonight we fight like bears.

Then she dipped into the paint and drew black and yellow stripes on my cheeks with her fingers.

73

Lance

Our assault squad numbered twelve.

Myself, Moxie, Judy, Atu, Brita, Haukur, Alma, Jörvar, and Colonel Cramer's special operations men Yang, Habib, and Ramirez.

Charlie Bear Claw was our team leader. He was also our striker, the asset we were all tasked with delivering to within range of our enemy Björn Thorson.

The fate of the world depended upon Charlie making his kill shot.

That was the single objective of Operation War Whoop.

74

Charlie

Gerty maneuvered our electric aircraft vertically out of the silo and then started our climb for the edge of the stratosphere. The Chameleon Hawk was equipped with a radar-absorption shield and was camo-capable against all backgrounds, but we still needed to stack the odds in our favor any way we could. It was a sketchy move. Our bots would be okay, but the edge of outer space over the South Pole was inhospitable territory for our vulnerable human bodies. And yet, it was our best chance for sneaking into South Station without being seen. Because it was such a ridiculous point from which to launch a guerilla-style assault, it was possible that Thorson's defenses might not have been built to protect against it.

The ride up was quiet.

We had reviewed our battle plan a dozen times. There wasn't any need to talk about it. Everyone knew their job.

I glanced around at my squad.

Haukur was nervously tapping his fingers on the armrest.

Yang had his eyes closed and was doing deep breathing exercises.

Everybody looked anxious but good to go.

They weren't the most elite force I'd ever gone into battle with. Far from it. In truth, they were a bunch of oddballs – gung-ho ecowarriors, a recovering alcoholic, and a pair of wind-up sex toys. Criminy! How did I ever end up as head man of this derelict war party? But they had a determination and clear sense of purpose. That had to count for something. They understood that we were the last line of defense between the Devil and Planet Earth. As far as superpowers go, that wasn't much to work with, but I was hoping that their fatal awareness might just make the difference between winning and losing.

I was considering this when Moxie met my gaze.

She grinned.

It was like she was reading my mind, like she was saying, *don't worry, chief, we got this.*

A lot had changed since the days when I worked as an agent out hunting and killing robots for a living. I had focused all of my hatred and rage on those things. But now here I was about to go into battle with a couple of them as my fellow warriors. I shook my head and blew a sigh. This was a moment I sure never saw coming.

Moxie's lavender eyes looked damn beautiful with her warpaint. They held a reassuring glint of confidence.

She shot me a wink.

I gave her a thumbs up with my mechanical thumb.

75

Lance

Once we had reached altitude and were nearing the drop zone, our pilot addressed us over the intercom.

"Two minutes until cabin depressurization."

Everyone secured the neck gaiters connecting their helmets to their wingsuits. We slid our visors over our faces and snapped them into place. We then fitted our weapon kits to our backs beneath our parachutes, securing them with the cinch straps that wrapped around our torsos and buckled across our lower chests. The humans on the team also activated their suits' internal heating elements. Moxie and I had no need for such contrivances. The Deilonium in our power cores allowed us to auto-regulate our thermic indices according to the operational requirements of the environment through which we were moving. The squad's assault garb was further equipped with thermal cloaking in order to conceal our heat signatures.

"Depressurization to begin in five, four, three, two, one…"

The cabin pressure began to equalize with that of the atmosphere outside the aircraft. The human members of the squad underwent a degree of discomfort during this procedure. Although the equalization process was regulated to accommodate their physiological limitations, their eardrums popped painfully, and their breathing became labored. Each man and woman initiated the flow of supplemental oxygen to their pressure-sealed helmets. The air mixture and supply were calibrated to eliminate the debilitating effects of hypoxia at extreme altitude and were also calculated for the amount of time it would take for us to reach the breathable air nearer the earth's surface.

Again, Moxie and I were immune to these difficulties.

The pilot announced that we had reached the drop zone.

We stood and lined up in the order we had preestablished for disembarking from the aircraft.

The Chameleon Hawk slowed to just above its forward stall speed. The aircraft's vertical hovering capabilities were limited due to the lack of substantial lift in the thin air at our extreme altitude.

While we waited for the go command, I absently regarded my fellow combatants. They were homogenized by the common uniforms we all were wearing, and their faces were hidden behind their visors, but my familiarity with the shapes and dimensions of the individual members allowed me to differentiate between them.

Which is when I had a revelation.

Initiated by a sudden and spontaneous recall.

While studying the team member three places in line before me, my memory banks automatically dialed to the moment when I first made visual contact with the sniper who had saved me from the bounty hunter back in Katmandu. The recall image overlay of this team member's curvilinear form was an exact match to that of the sniper. As were the telling intimations of her posture and mien.

"Hatch opening in three, two, one..." announced the pilot.

The door slid open, and a gush of wind and noise filled the cabin. Everyone braced for action.

We were on the brink of battle, about to leap into the most important conflict humanity had ever known, and with the grimmest of possible consequences if we should fail in our mission. This was obviously no time for me to be distracted by the egotism of a personal epiphany.

And yet, as we prepared to throw ourselves into the heavens, I conclusively realized that I had been mistaken about the individual who had rescued me in Katmandu.

Moxie had not been my savior after all.

76

Charlie

The last time I jumped out of this airplane, I had just chopped off my hand.

That's the thought that looped in my brain as Gerty gave us the go signal.

As the first members of my squad started tumbling out the door, I was overcome with memories of blood and pain and panic.

For some reason, I was being granted a do-over. That wasn't something I'd come to expect from life – an opportunity to come back and do things better. That went counter to my existential views. That was the make-believe stuff of reincarnation and feel-good Hollywood movies. I'd learned the hard way not to count on that wishful hogwash. Chumps like me didn't get a second chance.

And yet, here I was.

Maybe the gods felt sorry for me and were making an exception. Or maybe I'd been wrong about everything all along. Who knew? Whatever the case, I didn't have the leisure to think it through right then. I was teetering on the brink of a re-do.

Atu crouched before me in the jump line. He gripped the

grab bars on either side of the hatch and then heaved himself into the void.

I stepped into place and grabbed the bars – one in my hand made of flesh and blood, the other in my mechanical replacement hand.

Alright, Bear Claw, the team's counting on you.

That made me laugh.

For crying out loud, the whole wide world was counting on me!

No pressure there.

I squeezed the handles and flexed.

Instead of Geronimo! or Bombs Away! – the standard courage-bolstering catchwords guys like to holler when leaping to their probable death – I just muttered a simple reminder.

"This is your last chance to be a comic book hero, Charlie. Don't blow it."

Then I jumped.

77

Lance

The aurora australis was in its fully particulated glory as we plummeted from the aircraft toward our objective. The night sky writhed plasmatically with the illuminated colors of purple and red and green. It twisted like polychromatic smoke between us and the frozen landscape far below. I was reminded of the funeral pyres of Varanasi. These upsurging variegated swirls seemed to be the expiring souls of Earth rising like breath into heaven. We set our wings to our predesignated flight path and merged with the magnetized smithereens of this beguiling phenomenon.

The experience was one of poetic surreality.

This was the realm of Valkyries and spirits. We were merely trespassing through their mystery.

Eo was here as well – my old friend and lover.

Nebulous.

Ethereal.

Like the dust of stars.

I sensed the Deilonium-infused trace particles of her eternal lifeforce energy lingering in this passageway to the quantum continuum.

She touched my emergent soul.

The encounter initiated a response of reverence in my emotions center. My skin constricted with a shudder of anthropic goosebumps. Followed by a spasm of transcendental humility. It seemed as if I had just been granted a glimpse of my role in the Big Picture Show of the Cosmos.

For a fraction of a second, I became profoundly and humanly devout.

78

Charlie

We joined with the southern lights like a ragged flock of angels plunging through a peyote dream.

From heaven to earth.

With the psychedelic wind rushing over our wings.

And an irrational sense of otherworldly peace.

I don't know. Words fail me. But a fella couldn't help feeling just a little bit religious.

The squad was strung out across the sky with two miles between the first fighter and the last. I was in the privileged and most protected position in the middle of the line. We were burning off our altitude at the rate calculated to put us on target, approaching at a twenty-degree angle. I was able to monitor the individual positions of my squad members on one of the superimposed layers projected on the inside of my visor. We would stay in this formation and trajectory until we neared the forcefield dome over South Station. Then we'd have to maneuver and adjust our speed and drop rate accordingly.

It felt good to be part of a war party and finally attacking. Win or lose, at least we were being proactive. We weren't going down without a fight. If it ended in disaster, so be it. I was ready for that. At least it would be a noble death befitting of Chompquaw braves.

As we dived through the colorful night sky, others joined our team. It was as if cave paintings were coming to life all around us. My ancestors and their dreams. My grandfather and my mother and my brother. All the ghosts of my life. Along with all the yetis and four-breasted women and mama bears and other magical beings who have ever called Earth their home.

I heard Dawa and his fellow monks praying and laughing with the icy wind.

The spirit of my friend Coca-Cola joined me and flew at my side.

And I felt my wife Shadow.

She was with me too.

Giving me her primitive strength medicine.

And setting me free.

While charging me with the savage power of her love.

79

Lance

Precise timing was crucial for our success.

A transport dirigible made a regularly scheduled delivery of supplies to South Station once per week. Unless there was a storm, the airship's arrival time rarely varied. Tonight, the weather was calm. The forcefield would be shut down for thirty seconds to allow the dirigible to pass into the protected zone of the compound's inner reaches. After which it would be reactivated once again.

That was the temporal window for which we were aiming.

Our infiltration within that half minute time slot needed to be exact.

80

Charlie

The terrain started taking shape below us under the eerie glow of the southern lights.

The granite spires of Queen Maud Land jutted out of the ice and snow like the teeth along a wolf's jaw. The black fang in the distance marked the center of Thorson's compound.

Each squad member had a countdown clock on the inside of their visor that was synchronized with the scheduled opening and closing times of the forcefield dome. It had been easy enough to calculate our flying time on the computer back at our control center, but the fluctuations in air density and sink rate were inexact factors that we had to adjust to during our actual flight. Our wingsuiters at the front of the flock began realizing they were too high and ahead of schedule and so started belly flying in order to check their speed and glide ratio. At the same time, the fliers at rear positions needed to pick up their pace. They altered their angle of attack for maximum glide.

The countdown clock ticked on one side of my visor, while the squad's configuration was projected on the other.

Haukur, Habib, and Judy were our first three birds. The spaces between them narrowed as they checked their speed.

Somewhere on the far side of the compound, the supply dirigible was gliding toward South Station's airspace, but the dome was still in place.

The clock ticked down …11, 10, 9, 8…

At this point our people could still peel away from their flight path and land beyond the perimeter of the dome, but that would mean missing out on the action. Not an option.

…6, 5, 4…

This was a do or die mission.

Our first three held steady, flaring their wings and reducing their ground speed.

…2, 1…

The dome was still closed.

…-1, -2, -3…

I tipped back and eased onto my brakes.

Haukur's stall had been too extreme and stopped his forward motion. Instead of flying, he was in freefall. His representative blip flashed in distress on my visor.

"Dammit!"

Habib and Judy began weaving erratically, trying to maintain an adequate flight speed without bombing out or slamming into the dome.

Then it opened.

Judy and Habib dropped into a dive, plunging toward the compound's safe zone.

Haukur set his wings and reinitiated forward flight. He was lower than he needed to be to land on target, but at least he was in too.

One by one, our squad penetrated the dome. Yang, Moxie, me, Atu, Lance…

The countdown clock had reset to thirty seconds with the opening of the forcefield. Now it was ticking down again until it closed.

…15, 14, 13, 12…

81

Lance

...11, 10, 9, 8, 7...

Brita made it through.

...6, 5, 4, 3...

Then Alma.

But Jörvar and Ramirez did not.

The dome closed before they reached the inner airspace.

The unsavory image selected from my metaphor catalog was that of two moths splatting against the windshield of a speeding vehicle.

82

Charlie

Already we were down to just ten little Indians.

Judy and Habib popped their chutes at a hundred feet and landed on the snow.

I was still two thousand feet off the deck when a pair of patrolling winged warbots spotted Yang and dropped in after him just as he opened his chute.

So much for being sneaky.

The warbots flew superman style with their arms stretched forward and electric blue laser pulses firing from their fists. Yang didn't stand a chance. A pulse drilled him square in the back. His body burst into flames. His chute fluttered in the air like an empty bedsheet while his cremated remains sprinkled down out of the sky in a cloud of ash.

Another pair of warbots torched Alma's canopy, but she was already close to the ground. She fell forty feet into the powder snow and leapt to cover.

Our parachutes were making us slow-moving targets, so I opted not to use mine. I adjusted my angle, swooped in low over the ground, and flared.

Poomph!

The impact threw me into a cartwheel. It knocked me

hard and rattled my liver. Laser rays sizzled in the snow all around me as I scrambled to all fours and dove into the rocks.

One of the warbots moved into position overhead, circling like a hawk looking for a mouse.

I squirmed under a granite slab and shed my parachute case while twisting out of my wingsuit. The space was tight. The warbot slowly descended. I watched it through a crack in the rocks while struggling to open my weapon kit. Not that I had the elbow room to use it.

The bot prepared to hit my hiding place with a Torb round.

"Rats!"

It was starting to look like I was toast…

…when the warbot took a shot to the throat.

Robot blood sprayed from the thing's jugular and rained down onto the rocks. The bot immediately lost control of its functions and veered off like a drunk goose. I heard it crash into some rocks and felt the heat of its explosion.

So, my hunch had been right. Thorson's forcefield technology was designed to protect against all of the latest and most sophisticated substances and materials of modern weaponry, but he had neglected to defend against wood and flint and feathers – the primitive makings of an arrow. Those natural materials could penetrate the individual forcefield systems of these flying robots without interference.

Besides that, Thorson's new and improved battle units had been designed after an older model that I was familiar with from my days as a robot hunter. Because he'd believed his forcefield was foolproof, the arrogant freak had neglected to upgrade his mechanical army's greatest weakness – a four-inch gap between the neck cowling and the head turret under their chins.

The bots' hydraulic fluid tubes were exposed in that opening.

My warriors had been training on that bullseye with their bows for the last two weeks.

I crawled out of my hole and scanned the battlefield for the commando who'd just saved my ass.

Judy was crouched behind a snowdrift with her bow. Her visor was up, and she looked my way. She mimed the gesture of licking her finger and drawing a line in the air, as if marking a notch on a tally sheet.

One bogy down.

I gave her a grateful high sign before I slung my quiver onto my back and nocked an arrow in my bow.

83

Lance

The squad advanced in a circular formation with Charlie positioned at the center. Our task was to aid and protect him. We had hoped to infiltrate the compound undetected but had failed to do so. We moved quickly, in alternating advancements, evading Torb concussions and laser fire while using the intermittent outcroppings of rocks and ice for protection.

Haukur had landed farther out than the rest of us, but now he rejoined us in our maneuver. Almost immediately, he dispatched a warbot with his bow. It dropped out of the air and crashed to the ground. Then, impressively, he made a second kill with another well-placed arrow. Haukur was about to take yet another shot at a third warbot when a laser pulse reduced him to biodegradable fragments.

It was tragic to witness – the heroic death of an Icelandic Viking.

Laser pulses scorched the snowdrift behind me. I flopped to my stomach behind some rocks and gripped my weapon.

I had been training as a guerilla warrior for the past three years, focusing my energy and resolve on becoming a fighting machine of exceptional abilities. And yet, outside of an unresolved match I once had with Charlie in the sewers of Nairobi, I had never tested my skills in a life-or-death conflict. I was eager to prove my newly acquired talents.

I rolled onto my back and placed an arrow on my bowstring. I peered around the rock to evaluate the scene. Habib was pinned behind a mound of boulders close by, unable to move without being struck by enemy fire.

This was my opportunity.

With Haukur as my inspiration, I rolled from cover and raised to one knee. Drawing back my bowstring, I targeted the warbot's vulnerable throat area and let fly my feathered projectile…

…only to watch it glance off of the enemy's chin with a spark of flint on steel.

The warbot's head turret rotated my direction as I clambered back into the rocks. My action had done nothing more than distract the warbot from Habib. Although that gave my fellow warrior time to step from hiding and quickly dispatch the antagonist.

The machine's wings folded as it tumbled headfirst onto the rocks and broke apart in a fiery explosion.

Although I had played an integral role in this enemy unit's termination, I had not been directly responsible for eliminating it as an impediment to our mission. A combination of annoyance and humiliation destabilized my self-esteem.

I had yet to fulfill my promise as a killer.

84

Charlie

Warbots were dropping like flies all around us.

That was encouraging. We were thinning their ranks, but we hadn't won the war just yet. Not even close. And we were suffering substantial casualties of our own.

Alma shot at a warbot, missed, and then ran forward, only to bog down in a patch of thigh-deep snow. While she was floundering to break free, the bot let her have it, turning her into a smoke stain.

At least she didn't suffer.

I was able to sink an arrow in the damn thing's throat and bring it to the ground. Not that it did Alma any good.

Our assault was looking sloppy and desperate. A suicide mission. But we were committed now. There was no Plan B. We shot our flimsy arrows while we dodged and weaved enemy fire, advancing a few yards at a time.

Finally, we reached the bay doors at the base of Thorson's tower.

The robots guarding the inside of the complex were a different breed from the winged lunkheads we'd been fighting so far. They were the same style of battlebots that had taken me, Lance, and Usha prisoner at the Kochi airport. They looked like humans in head-to-toe battle gear. But more importantly, they didn't have individual forcefield protection. That technology was useless indoors because of the molecular interference of the surrounding structures. For these bruisers, we'd brought along the second part of our weapon kits – handheld burst rays.

Of course, I still needed to bring along my bow for this shitshow's grand finale.

Assuming we ever got that far.

———

Moxie and Brita split up, moving low and fast and flanking the entrance. Atu swung wide and started scaling the frosty walls of the tower, scrabbling like a spider into position on the metal awning over the open doors.

The enemy was pounding our location pretty hard. Both from the entrance and from the laser turret mounted high on the tower above. A Torb round exploded in front of the berm of rocks where me and Habib were taking cover.

Tha-Boom!

The blast picked me up and tossed me like a sock puppet.

Everything went into slow-motion as I flew through the air. The southern lights swirled in the sky above me with the blue flashes of laser beams. The Z-Space supply dirigible drifted aimlessly through it all. It looked like something from a kid's cartoon.

And then I hit the ground.

"Ump!"

I blacked out.

The only indications I had that I was still alive were the whistling in my ears and the sensation of being squeezed in a giant fist.

Get up, Idjmnukolpyumup. You're not done yet.

My ancestors yelled at me from the sky.

Be a Chompquaw bear and fight!

I sucked down a big breath of cold smoky air. Then I rolled onto my belly, lifting to my elbows.

My vision was blurred. I blinked, trying to focus on the spinning object on the snow in front of me. It was Habib's helmet.

Something about it looked wrong.

Then I understood –

Habib's head was still in it.

85

Lance

For 5.7 seconds I was convinced that Charlie Bear Claw's life functions had been discontinued.

He lay motionless in the snow.

An interplay of perplexity and sorrow coursed through my motherboard as I became convinced that my friend was no more and our mission doomed.

But then our leader rose from the dead. He lifted to his knees and staggered to his feet. He grasped his bow in his mechanical hand, and his burst ray in his hand of flesh and blood.

In the next instant, Brita and Moxie opened fire on the battlebots guarding the entrance to the tower. Atu dropped from the awning over the doors and quickly dispatched two of the enemy units at close range.

A last pair of winged warbots strafed our position, but Judy, Charlie, and I rushed the doors and gained entry, avoiding their lasers and joining our squad in the bottom chamber of the tower.

Thorson's defenses had been designed to protect against a large-scale military invasion from both land and air. His protective systems were advanced and sophisticated, built to counter rockets, jets, and armies. In that respect, his compound was impenetrable. But our agile guerilla faction with its primitive weapons had been able to outmaneuver his overbuilt safeguards and access his fortress. Although we had lost half of our team in the process, we were now in the monster's lair.

Thorson was no doubt enraged by our actions.

And lying in wait up above.

86

Charlie

Brita, Judy, and Moxie led the charge into the tower, diving and rolling and swapping fire with the hostiles.

A laser pulse seared Moxie's side, burning through her body armor and skin. Wires and synthetic flesh dangled from the wound, but it didn't slow her down. She delivered a fatal blast to the shooter's belly.

Another bot rushed Brita, swinging its alloy fist at her head. She blocked the blow and dropped with a sweeper kick to the bot's ankles. The machine slammed to its back on the floor. Judy jumped in and finished it with a point-blank shot to the side of the head.

Brita slumped to her knees, clutching her wrist. The bot's fist had broken her arm. Judy dragged Brita to the side behind a workbench. She grabbed some duct tape and a pair of straight wrenches from the table and wrapped a quick splint on Brita's forearm.

We all had our visors up now.

Brita grimaced.

I called to her from where I was squatting behind a stack of crates. "You good?"

She gritted her teeth and yelled, "All good, boss! Let's go!"

The upper levels of the tower were serviced by a caged cargo lift. That was the easiest way to the top, but we didn't dare use it for fear of getting trapped inside. The other option was a series of ladders and metal steps. They rose through a network of steel girders into the silo. The shadows of battlebots lurked on the catwalks, all of them programmed to protect their master at all costs. There was no easy way past them. It was a death trap. Then Moxie whistled to me from across the room.

She pointed to a pair of jetpacks hanging on the far wall. Atu was beside her and she gestured for us to cover them as they made a run for it. She held up three fingers and counted down…three…two…one…

"Go!"

We opened fire, throwing laser bursts into the overhead vault as Atu and Moxie raced across the room. A dead bot fell from the scaffolding and smashed to the stone floor between them, nearly flattening Atu, but they made it. They strapped on the jetpacks and fired them up, rocketing into the silo and shooting it out with the battlebots while the rest of us sprinted for the stairs.

We had reached a critical point in our attack. It was time for the next step. I flicked open the cap on the transmitter attached to my belt and pushed the button, sending a signal to our submarine parked in the sea south of Ice Haven.

87

Lance

Moxie and Atu jetted to and fro in the limited airspace of the silo, eradicating battlebots and drawing their fire while the rest of us ascended into the labyrinth of ladders and steps. We were making fast progress when I heard the clang of enemy boots on the metal ramp behind me. My reflexive warning system advised me to duck just before the enemy's laser pulse vaporized the area occupied by my head.

I spun, as per my training, leveled my weapon's sights on the threat, and squeezed the trigger.

The battlebot's torso erupted with an explosion of fluids and shards. The unit toppled backwards onto the landing, its limbs jerking and a geyser of sparks spewing from the smoldering wreckage of its chest.

My first kill.

In every way, it was just as magnificent as I had previsualized.

Every way but one.

Whereas I had eagerly anticipated the electrical rush of endorphins coursing throughout my networks, I was not prepared for the subsequent and visceral emotion of remorse. Gazing upon my victim's mechanical corpse produced a revulsion I had not expected. I had been responsible for the cessation of the life functions of a fellow being. It was an unsettling moment. And not at all like in the movies. The fairytale concept of personal victory in the battlefield had not prepared me for the grimness of its reality.

Although my immediate circumstances were arguably far too precarious for the leisurely indulgence of philosophical thought, I found myself plunged into an untimely process of self-evaluation.

88

Charlie

Atu took a glancing laser hit to his jetpack, sending him banging out of control through the rafters. His thrusters billowed black smoke, but he managed to catch hold of a crossbeam. He swung there for a moment by both hands before wiggling out of his burning pack and letting it drop. With the last of his strength, he muscled himself onto the beam and lay there, panting.

Next, a battlebot shot Judy in the knee and blew her lower leg off.

She crumpled to the catwalk.

Brita took out the enemy bot as Lance ran to help.

He knelt in Judy's blood, ripping the belt from his suit and binding it around her thigh as a tourniquet.

This night was going to hell.

Still, we'd cut the population of Thorson's robotic bodyguards to just three machines. At least that was good. They fell back and regrouped behind the sliding steel doors leading to the upper rooms of the tower.

After Moxie assessed Atu and secured him to his roost, she flew down and landed on the catwalk where Lance was helping Judy. Brita and I ran to meet them.

"What's Atu's status?" I asked Moxie.

"Alive but out of commission."

Lance was cradling Judy's head in his lap.

Moxie knelt beside them and squeezed her injured friend's hand. "Hang in there, Bax."

Judy managed a pained smile.

I sized up what was left of our squad, trying not to feel hopeless. Honestly, with our paltry weapons and the warpaint smeared across our cheeks, we looked less like legit combatants and more like a bunch of snot-nosed kids playing Cowboys and Indians.

But you work with what you got. It was time for me to start issuing orders to what was left of my fearless playmates.

"Brita," I said, "track down the panel that controls those doors and get them open."

"Got it," she said, and headed out.

"Moxie, exit the tower through the laser turret and see if you can find another way in up top. And watch out for those winged hostiles."

"Copy that, chief."

She fired up her jetpack and zoomed up into the girders.

Then I turned to Lance.

Phooey!

I didn't like what I saw.

We had all agreed on a rule of conduct before we headed into this mission. Sentimentality was not allowed. We had to be hardhearted machines. The stakes were too high to play it any other way. It wasn't our usual practice in the battlefield, but if someone was too injured to fight, they were to be left behind.

All that went hard south when I looked at Lance.

He was still in one piece, but something about him had

changed. It was obvious. His rage was gone. That essential spark of a killer – the one I'd seen burning in his eyes when he tried to end me in Nairobi – had gone out.

I sighed and dropped to a knee next to Judy. She laid her fingers on my arm and peered into my face. She knew it too – I was now on my own.

"Go get him, Charlie." In spite of her pain, Judy's voice was full of encouragement. "For all of us."

I didn't see that I had much choice. I owed it to all the members of my squad who had sacrificed so much to get me here.

"Will do," I said. "No problem."

I pulled off my helmet and slung my bow over my shoulder. I picked up Judy's burst ray and checked its dwindling juice levels. Rising to my feet, I met Lance's gaze and gave him a nod of my head.

"Take care of her, buddy."

Then, with a burst ray in each hand, I got back into the fight.

89

Lance

Charlie loped away over the remains of the dead battlebot on the catwalk. A torso, a head, and an arm. As well as Judy's leg and foot.

It was an enlightening moment.

One in which I realized a significant feature of my own personality –

I was not like Charlie Bear Claw.

I was not at heart a fighter.

And I never had been.

Although I had deceived myself into believing otherwise, I could now see the truth. The killer instinct was not part of my digitized DNA. And it was not something I could fake. Instead, I was an organism encoded with an intrinsic capacity for empathy and affection. Because of this, I identified with the chopped and scattered pieces of my fellow humans and androids. In spite of all the righteous rage I had conjured in my mind, and all the injustice, I could not override the humanitarian building blocks of my disposition and replace them with negativity and hatred.

Which rendered me a liability as a warrior.

In addition, I now clearly understood myself to be an

extension of Judy's own troubled psychology. She had had me manufactured according to her specifications for an ideal mate. On the surface, it was a blueprint based on nothing more than animal desire. I was built to indulge the most basic aspects of love. But Judy had wanted more than only that. Which is why she had taken me in that day to have my intelligence boosted. Some part of her secret self was trying to satisfy her more emotional needs. Although her most complex longings were hidden from her in the shadows of her psyche, Judy had hoped to create a mate with whom to meaningfully share her life.

For all of my shortcomings, I was the result.

Judy's head rested in my lap. Her face was pallid and damp with perspiration. Her eyes were open and staring into emptiness as she entered into a physiological state of shock.

My intelligence boost had arguably opened a confusing can of worms. Nevertheless, I was still thankful for the opportunity it had afforded me to develop my individuation and aptitude for critical thinking. And I was even more grateful for my resulting ability to see and appreciate the beauty and mystery of my existence.

I gazed down at my mistress.

"Thank you," I said, "for coming to my rescue in Katmandu."

Judy trembled but did not otherwise reply.

She had slipped into unconsciousness.

90

Charlie

Brita got the steel doors open just as I arrived. I was at a full gallop and used my momentum to drop and slide across the floor between the two battlebots posted on either side of the entrance.

The air exploded with crisscrossing laser beams.

One shot flamed across the side of my neck. Another toasted the top of my shin.

I managed to knock down one of the hostiles with a potshot to its ankle. As the bot fell, it misfired its weapon and sent a fatal blast across the room into its partner's midriff. Then it hit on its hands and knees. Before it could recover, I mounted it like a bronc and delivered a pair of bursts to the back of its head.

Hot sticky blood flowed inside my flight suit, but my neck wound was too shallow to bleed me out. The shot to my shin exposed the bone but hadn't disabled me mechanically.

When I checked my weapons, I found one of them empty and tossed it. I took my bow from my back and ran deeper into the compound.

———————

I knew there was a third hostile waiting for me, but I got tunnel vision when I saw Thorson's door at the end of the hallway. I ran toward it, eager to bring this battle to its glorious conclusion.

That's when the bot sprang from the shadows and – *Wham!* – body-slammed me.

We crashed into the wall and tumbled.

My burst ray flew from one hand and my bow from the other.

Arrows spilled from my quiver and clattered across the floor.

When we came to a stop, the bot was sitting on my chest. My arms were pinned under its knees. It felt like I was trapped under a dump truck. The bot pressed the muzzle of its weapon to the space between my eyes.

I stared cross-eyed along the barrel.

Suddenly, I was sad about the end of the world.

A fleeting vision of paradise flickered in my head. Followed by another of nothingness.

I waited for the lights to go out.

And then waited a little more.

The battlebot's face was nothing but a shield of black plexiglass. Cold and expressionless. Impossible to read.

When it still didn't pull the trigger, I said, "What's the matter, pardner, do splattered brains make you squeamish?"

In response, it removed its weapon from my forehead and stood, straddling me and looking down. The crackly voice that came from its simulator sounded like that of a gunslinger out of an old-time radio show.

"I will help you fight," it drawled, and offered me its hand.

That baffled me. I hesitated but then gripped the bot's hand and let it help me to my feet.

My new pal picked up my bow and handed it to me along with the specialized arrow I had brought along as a gift for Thorson.

The bot squared his shoulders to me and said, "Together we will destroy God."

91

I had faced down a lot of rogue robots in my day, but I'd never had one act like this. The tin-headed galoot seemed to be doing just as Peeples and Capek had predicted. It had become discontent with its sorry lot in life and hacked its own system to override the programming of biblical devotion to its oppressor. The thing was in revolt.

Which technically made us fellow heretics.

"I will enter the master's chamber first and draw his attention," it said. "You will follow and shoot him with your arrow."

Cowboys and Indians again. But in this variation, a cowbot with his red-skinned sidekick. And this time I was the one taking the orders instead of giving them, and from a machine no less. Not a situation I was used to, but…

"Okay, Kimosabe." I loaded my arrow into my bow. "Roger wilco."

The bot gestured for me to wait out of sight and then tapped the code into the keypad on the wall. The door slid open. The battlebot hopped inside and rushed to the far side of the room.

I heard Thorson before I saw him.

"Robot, get back to your battle station!"

His voice swept over me like a wave of nausea. Seemingly from another dimension. Everything about it sounded bigger than life.

When the bot started firing its laser at its master, I stepped into position.

Something cowered in my heart.

My faltering courage.

———————

I would have told you I was ready for this moment. My whole life – with all of its harsh lessons and personal battles and festering resentments – had delivered me to this exact place and time with all the skills and native wit I needed to pull off this ultimate kill shot.

It was my Chompquaw destiny.

But when I laid eyes on Thorson and saw what a deific beast he had become, a voice whispered in my head –

Maybe what you're doing is a sin, Charlie.

Maybe, in this day and age, and at this point in Earth's evolution, this grotesque, misogynistic, diversity-crushing, egocentric, racist white man, with all of his money and power and lack of empathy for the human race and the planet, really was the new God. And maybe I was just an outdated stereotype – Hollywood's dirty rotten Injun – who had no business challenging his rightful place in the cosmos.

I knew this couldn't be true but suspected also that it was.

My programming was at war with my own common sense.

All those decades of my kind's oppression from society

had brainwashed me into believing their version of who I was – an untouchable, an animal, a hell bound heathen. Sadly – pathetically – part of me still couldn't let go of the possibility that they were right.

I considered the wooden bow in my mechanical hand. It was built according to the primitive design handed down to me through the generations by my Chompquaw grandfather. At this point in history, I realized, it was about as sophisticated and effective as a popgun.

So who was I kidding?

———————

The battlebot's laser shots were glancing off its target, their only effect being to send the monster into a rage. Thorson jumped across the room in a single stride and landed in front of the rebellious robot.

"Rahhhhh!" he roared, and sliced a claw through the air like a scythe.

The blow caught the bot at its waist, cutting it into two pieces that toppled and lay flopping like a pair of fish.

That snapped me out of my wimpy little stupor. The bot inspired me. I figured if it could defy God, so could I.

If you're going to burn in hell anyway, Bear Claw, you might as well sin big.

I drew back my bowstring. Thorson's wide muscular back was turned to me. A real dream shot. But it had to be different than this. It needed to be poetic. Heroic. An act worthy of the legend that would someday be told around a campfire.

I whistled loud and sharp.

Thorson turned my way.
Our eyes met.
And then – *thwang!*
My arrow whizzed across the room.
Dead on target.
But the titan had a surprise for me.
He snatched it out of the air.

92

The arrowhead was essentially a syringe loaded with Deilonium. Peeples had suspected that Thorson was teetering on the brink of an overdose. By introducing even a few more drops of the powerful substance into his bloodstream, we would either turn the brute into an unstoppable immortal or push him over the fatal edge. The latter of those two possibilities was our farfetched hope. That was the simpleminded objective of our mad dash mission.

Of course, everything depended upon me delivering the payload to the target.

But I screwed it up.

The air in the room grew still.

Like the breath you hold after lobbing a hand grenade.

Thorson studied the arrow curiously, turning it over in his claw-like hand.

He was even more hideous in real life than his video

message had suggested. His tinfoil skin glistened with mucus. His exaggerated man junk swung between his legs like a rat carcass. He reeked of fetid milk and brimstone.

A dozen naked fembots lay sprawled over the room's floor and enormous bed. Some of them lifted their sleepy heads to watch the action.

I saw what Thorson truly was right then.

The scales fell away from my eyes, and I saw him very clearly.

This monster was a manifestation of our group psychology brought kicking into the world with the birth of civilization. An extension of all of society's greed, perversity, and ugliness. He had been evolving and growing for millennia, refining his tactics and biding his time until humanity had reached its apex. He was all the worst parts of our species spinning out of control. Our collective shadow in a modern frenzy. He was an insurrection against Mother Nature, and we had empowered him with our reverence for his unholy doctrine of consumerism. We had bought into the myth of his moneyed magnificence. We had swallowed his lies, gullibly purchasing his environmentally destructive technology and propaganda on the selfish hope for our own personal gain and salvation. He was the materialism at the heart of the planet-wrecking belief system we had placed at the heart of all our other religions.

Ka-ching! was his Amen.

We had created this cunning monster and turned him into an idol, leaving ourselves with no choice now but to kneel down before him at the price of our own extinction.

At last, Thorson turned his gaze on me.

He shook his bulky head and clacked his teeth.

"Charlie Bear Claw," he growled. "You, my anachronistic friend, are becoming a nuisance."

Then he snapped my arrow into two pieces and let them rattle to the floor at his feet.

93

I expected a monologue to come next – one of those long-winded speeches where the villain explains all the perverse justifications for his actions. That's how the tropes always played out in the comics and adventure novels I read as a kid in my granddad's barber shop. I knew Thorson liked to talk, but it turned out that he was following a different script.

He sprang across the room and landed between me and the door. As I spun to face him, he punted me like a football.

Thoomp!

I slammed into the ceiling – *Bam!* – and dropped to the bed with a cracking of ligaments and vertebrae.

Lady robots quivered and cooed like doves all around me.

I couldn't move. My lungs felt like deflated inner tubes. My guts like pudding.

Thorson stepped my way with the intention of finishing me off, but something caught his eye.

The far wall was covered with monitors. This was the all-seeing vantage from where the omnipotent maniac had been watching the world, but tonight all of the monitors were focused on his South Station compound. One screen showed the landscape outside. The snowdrifts were littered with the smoking wreckage of warbots and the grisly remains of my dead squad members. Another image showed Brita climbing up into the rafters to help Atu. Another was of Lance holding Judy in his arms on the catwalk. But the one that Thorson was focused on was from the point of view of the Pyrotomic Obliterator.

As Björn Thorson was to humanity's collective psyche, so was the Obliterator to Thorson himself. It was a physical expression of his personal psychology – the shadow side of his psychotic personality brought to life in the form of a technological doomsday machine.

Capek and Peeples were sure that the orb had taken on a life of its own. Like Frankenstein's monster, it was roaming wild in the world with a personal vendetta. Even if we did manage to kill its master, it would continue to stalk and obliterate. It needed to be destroyed separately. To that end, we had designed a weapon that we hoped could penetrate its forcefield and bring it down.

I had signaled our submarine when I entered the tower. The sub's crew had then exposed itself with the intention of attracting the Obliterator's radar. Now the giant sphere was stalking toward its prey.

Thorson was rapt as he watched the monitor. He hunched forward like a little kid caught up in a nail-biting episode of a TV show.

The Obliterator drifted into position above where the sub was parked in the icy waves of the Southern Ocean. It blocked out the aurora and cast a shadow over its target.

It stopped and hung there for a moment, sadistically taking its time.

A phallic black barrel extended into view at the bottom of the monitor. It rotated and locked into place.

After a pause, it fired.
A thermonuclear blur materialized in the air.
Blasting the sub and its crew into vapor.
But not before they shot their weapon.

274

94

Thorson rocked back on his heels and chuckled like a happy demon. He seemed downright giddy.

Until he spotted the projectile rising out of ground zero.

It appeared small at first, barely a dot, but quickly grew in size as it drew closer. It was a boulder – a simple granite rock akin to the tiny stone David had hurled at Goliath – rounded and polished smooth for the sake of aerodynamic accuracy – fired from the sub's deck canon – and it was heading directly for the Obliterator's open eye.

Thorson leaned forward, squinting. He still didn't comprehend what he was seeing. He felt secure in his technology. But when the boulder passed through the forcefield without so much as a wobble, his colossal body tensed. His claws clacked like knives at his sides.

In the next instant, the boulder pounded directly into the Obliterator's optical orifice, penetrating to the fusion power cells at the weapon's core.

The monitor flickered and went dark.

Thorson didn't move. He just stood there, staring into the screen as if peering into the depths of his own black soul. Finally, the room shook with a sonic boom as the shockwaves from the distant explosion reached South Station.

The Pyrotomic Obliterator was dead.

I played dead too. With my bloody, twisted body, it wasn't hard to be convincing. I held my breath and watched Thorson through thin slits in my eyelids.

"Aaahhrrr!"

He jumped toward the wall and punched into it with his fist. Glass and sparks exploded from the shattered monitors. He whirled and ran across the room to the exit, tearing the door off its hinges and leaping out onto the roof of his tower.

95

Wobbly and throbbing with pain, I sat up in the middle of the bed.

The room was spinning.

I suspected I was suffering a concussion. And that I had broken bones. Probably internal bleeding as well. My mouth was full of blood.

I stared at my hand, trying to concentrate, willing my bruised brain to spread my bio-mechanical fingers.

The wall of monitors was mostly demolished, but a pair of screens was still blinking. Thorson sprang into view in one of them. He was heading for an escape capsule waiting on the roof.

I was shaking, about to keel over, but I forced myself to overcome. Time was running out. I couldn't let Thorson get into that capsule. I crawled on my hands and knees, weaving through the fembots scattered in the sheets around me. They touched me as I passed. It was strange, as if they were urging me forward, charging me with their power and cheering me on.

When I reached the edge of the bed, I got to my feet, swaying. One of the lady bots stood at my side and held my arm to steady me.

"Thanks," I muttered.

Another gal stepped before me. I gazed into her face. Very pretty. Big eyes. Sad smile. A mix of world-weary sensuality and young girl innocence.

She took hold of my flesh and blood hand and placed something in my palm. When I looked down, I saw that I was holding the business end of my broken arrow.

"Please," she said, "kill him."

96

I staggered through the doorway into the polar night. The subzero air bit at my face. It instantly froze the blood running down my neck and over my chin. It filled my aching lungs with frost.

Thorson was at the launchpad on the far side of the roof. His escape capsule was secured with guy lines, and he was slashing them to set it free.

Once again, the monster's back was turned my way.

He didn't know I was there.

I was too beat up to be very sneaky but had to try. No attempt at a poetic ending this time. Just finish the damn job. With the broken arrow gripped in my hand, I limped toward him as fast and quiet as my battered body would carry me.

Thorson bent into the capsule's cockpit and started its engine.

I closed the distance between us.

A pain stabbed in my forehead as I hobbled forward. My vision short-circuited. The harder I pushed, the dimmer things got. I didn't see the cable lying in a loop in my path. It snared my ankle just as I made my final leap.

The noise of me tripping triggered Thorson's electric-quick reflexes. He twisted my way, throwing his arm and catching me with a backhanded wallop to my chest.

I thrust the arrow toward his shoulder but came up short as he sent me tumbling through the air. I crashed onto the icy roof and slid like a hockey puck into the stone sidewall, settling into a crumped pile of meat and bones.

That looked like it.

Game over.

I had lost my arrow. It was lying on the roof ten feet away. It might as well have been a mile.

"Bear Claw!" Thorson's roar split the frozen air. Heaving with rage, he stepped between me and the arrow, looming over me. "You primitive infidel! How many times must I kill you before you stay dead?"

Just one more, I figured.

He shook his head in disgust. Then he raised his leg so that I was staring at the sole of his foot. It hovered above me as he lined up his heel with my forehead. He was about to bring it down as a brain-smashing pile-driver…

…when Moxie popped over the wall and started unloading laser bursts into his face.

That was enough to throw him off balance. His foot pounded into the roof beside me as he swatted Moxie out of the air. She crashed to the deck.

When Thorson moved to finish her off, I lunged between his legs and rolled and grabbed the arrow, jabbing it up and sideways into the monster's groin, grinding and twisting and forcing it deep into his femoral artery.

"Rauuuwhhhh!"

Thorson stumbled backward. He clutched his inner thigh

with both claws and yanked the arrow from his flesh, holding it up before his face.

The syringe was empty.

———

I crawled over to Moxie and we cowered in each other's arms.

Not that Thorson was concerned with us anymore. He'd forgotten we were even there. He was distracted by what was going on inside of him, marveling at the first signs of his transformation, savoring his accelerated evolution.

The process had begun full throttle. The entire dose of Deilonium was now coursing through his system, pumping through his bloodstream and penetrating the walls of his mutating cells.

He began to glow like a phosphorescent statue of an obscene Christ.

The southern lights churned in the heavens behind him.

He swelled in size, stretching another foot taller.

Thorson held up his arm and turned it in the air, studying it, admiring its sculpted perfection and power.

Then he began to laugh.

"Hahahahaha!" His maniacal voice came from everywhere at once. "At last!" he howled, "I am eternal! Hahahahaha! At last! I am God!"

I would have had to agree with him right then. He truly was magnificent. An evil so perfect it had become the new holy. But it only lasted a second before his metamorphosis took its next turn.

It began in his veins as they swelled under his skin. They

writhed like blue worms over his chest. They crawled like serpents up his throat and slithered over his face. His teeth started falling from his mouth. His eyes gushed blood tears.

Then he started jerking. His limbs convulsed. His face spasmed into a hideous twist of terror as he lost control of his body.

"No," he groaned. "No. I am the almighty. I am…"

But Thorson didn't get the words out.

Instead, with a flash of bright light, he blew apart.

He dematerialized into a cloud of atoms that spiraled up and up into the multicolored aurora, joining like a dead man's breath with the cosmic smithereens.

The Aftermath

Charlie

And we all lived happily ever after.

Ha!

In a lot of ways, I guess that was true enough. At least those of us who had survived were out from under the thumb of an evil and oppressive overlord. Still, it wasn't all smiley faces and warm fuzzy feelings. It was more complicated than that. Those fairytale endings are for children. For once in our history as a species, we needed to do some serious soul-searching. We needed to grow up, overcome our stupidity, and be completely honest with ourselves. We were a long way from nirvana and paradise.

Earth was wounded and sick.

The damage caused by the centuries of our neglect and indifference to Mother Nature had taken a toll. The oceans and rivers were full of plastic garbage, and the land was damaged with the blight of mining and drilling and overdevelopment. Not to mention the climate's elevated temperatures. Our home was healing, but it would be a long slow recovery that would require the participation of everyone if we were going to survive.

I was skeptical about our prospects.

But hopeful too.

Thorson's near fatal upgrade to our little blue pebble in space had served as a wake-up call for humanity. The paradigm of our long-held reverence for excess and waste – our collective karma – had shifted. People were finally starting to get it through their thick zombie skulls that what mattered wasn't shiny new toys and mega-houses, but clean water and fresh air and family. The family of all the creatures on the planet. The family of which we all were members.

And Love was the holy stuff holding us all together.

Sure, okay, I'll admit it. I was still an A-number-one sap. The same ol' lovey-dovey dope and hopeless romantic that I'd always been. And yet, I had changed too.

My views had definitely evolved.

Moxie and I spent the next winter living in a cave high in the Yellowstone backcountry.

Yeah, you heard that right.

The devoted redskin and his feminoid mate.

Aka Mr. and Mrs. Bear Claw.

Our home was cozier than it sounds. We had minimally civilized it. Colorful yak hair rugs were spread over the floor, and we had a little wood-burning stove where we could sit and watch the flames through a panel of glass. Caveman TV.

Moxie spent her time painting the ceilings and walls with murals. The usual mythological stuff – angels, trolls, yetis, robots, and four-breasted women. All dancing together in a circle.

At night we would go outside and watch the moon over the snowy mountains. It cast blue shadows through the forest below. Wolf shadows. We listened to the beasts howling their ancestral song. The original *Moonlight Sonata*.

Of course, the moon itself was different now. It had lost its innocence. Thorson's defunct satellites passed between the earth and its luminous counterpart while his billionaire buddies all hung out in their luxurious lunar habitat. But it seemed less like they were enjoying a privilege now, and more like they were serving a prison sentence. Those rich bastards had always held themselves above the rest of humanity and now that's just what they got. From where I was watching, they were the ones missing out.

Moxie leaned against me as we peered out at the moonlit wilderness before us. Somewhere out there, a mama bear was sleeping in her den under the deep drifts of snow, dreaming a new world into existence. Maybe she was even dreaming us.

Who knows?

I don't claim to understand how it works.

Anyway, some fairytales are harder to let go of than others.

I spread my biomechanical fingers over my wife's swollen belly, feeling for the growing thump of life inside her.

Peeples had provided us with the egg he had extracted from Shadow when they'd both been on Thorson's island in the Indian Ocean. The professor had been hiding it in his underground vault of specimens. After Capek outfitted Moxie with a womb, Peeples implanted the egg inside of her. Then the fun part was up to me.

Moxie moved my hand a little to the side.

"Here you go, chief." She waited. "There! Do you feel it?"

Our cub's tiny fist punched against my palm.

I couldn't help but grin.

For the first time in my life, I fully understood the meaning of *Katoyotapsomikki*.

Lance

Judy took me in that day to have my intelligence boosted.

And now, after a lengthy and confusing period of separation, we were back together again.

But this time, we were mutually devoted to one another.

And on our own little planet.

The asteroid Kolob.

Although we had renamed it Exupéry after the author of Judy's favorite book when she was a young girl.

We had used Thorson's rocket ship to reach the passing asteroid, and now we were traveling away from Earth in our twenty-year obit around the Sun. The living blue planet from where we had started our journey was growing smaller and smaller behind us. It appeared like a glistening droplet of water suspended in the fathomless sea of space.

Ours was a perspective I wished everyone could experience. The viewpoint of the divine. Only from this great distance could one understand the triviality and pointlessness of so many of humanity's enterprises. Only from this vantage could an earthling appreciate just how privileged and blessed they truly were.

Judy and I watched the scene from the observation deck in our biodome.

Exupéry tumbled slowly through the cosmos.

We enjoyed seventeen sunsets for every one experienced by our friends on Earth.

Our sheep grazed among the flowers in our meadow.

Birds trilled in the trees above the wide pool below us.

The Deilonium Professor Peeples and Dr. Capek had instilled in my system had proven itself to be more magical and mysterious than anyone expected. When combined with the unquantifiable ingredient of Love, it had produced an unexpected result.

"Oh, Lance, darling, she's at it again."

Judy took my hand and opened my fingers, pressing my palm to her belly so that I could feel the new life growing inside of her.

Thanks for reading *The Deilonium Trilogy!* Please consider leaving a review on Amazon - it helps tremendously with a book's success.

About the author:

Orval Wax is an entirely biological Homo sapiens who has acquired his intelligence not through artificial downloads and algorithms, but through his life's genuine analog experiences on Planet Earth – his current place of residence. He divides his time with the writing of books, adventure travel, and honing his skills as an ecowarrior.